Training My Professor

Thimble

Training My Professor
Thimble

Published by Boy Howdy Publications

Books by Thimble

When Femdom Dreams Come True
Training My Professor

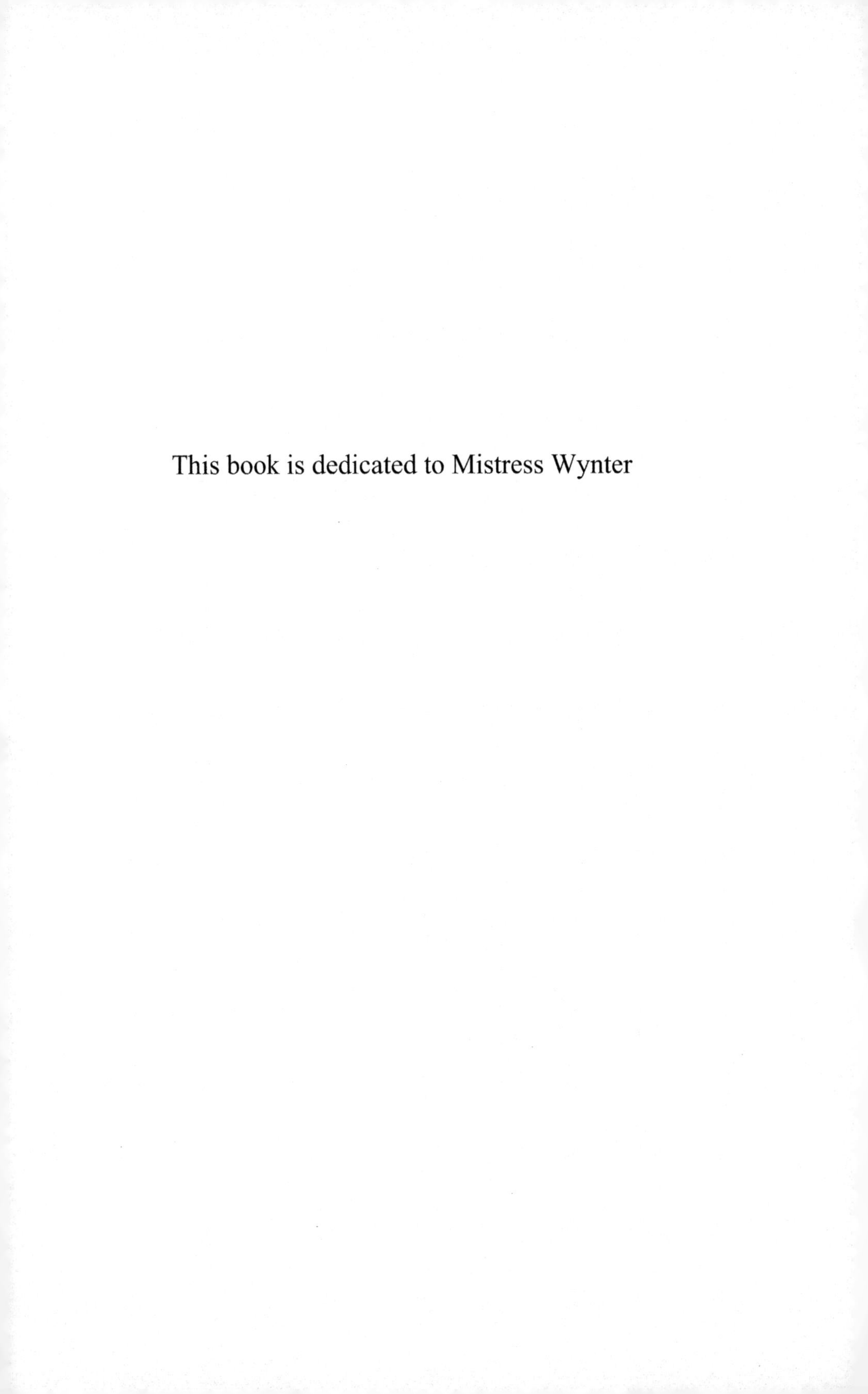

This book is dedicated to Mistress Wynter

Chapter 1

My name is Taylor Clark. I'm a 33 year-old Psychology professor at Clareville University. This is my fourth year at the school and it would be a crime if I didn't receive tenure in the Spring. I've published nine articles in respected journals since I started here, all of which were received well, and one of which was republished in a best-of-the-year compilation: the cover of which is framed and hanging in my office.

I know I sound cocky, but I was a mediocre student who couldn't sit still and was told by more than one teacher that I'd never amount to anything. I limped through high school and only got into college because of an athletic scholarship. But there, everything changed thanks to Dr. Patricia West, my social psychology professor. For the first time, I was interested in an academic subject, and for the first time a professor told me I had potential. She also told me I was lazy, had a bad attitude and needed to work harder, but it was so clearly done with support and respect that I listened. I loved feeling like I was a valuable member of class: I'd never felt that way before. I worked hard, and with Dr. West's help, I got into a good grad school, where I got my PhD. Now I'm a professor. None of my high school teachers would believe it.

I love my job. I love supporting students the way Dr. West supported me. I see it as my responsibility to prepare students both academically and emotionally for the world after college.

Physically, I'm 6'1" with short dark hair and broad shoulders. In the words of my publicist, who is given to exaggeration, I'm ruggedly handsome and manly, which

I don't deny has helped me land me a growing number of television appearances. My specialty is motivation and manipulation, so whenever some crazy cult leader makes the news, I'm brought in to explain how people end up enslaving themselves to him. The truth is usually that these are weak people with little else in their lives, but I try to sugarcoat it a little.

It was morning, two days before the start of school, and I had a meeting with two new transfer-student advisees and some research to do for a new book that I'd been putting off for about a month. I would need to eat and take a shower, but first I had to deal with Mandy, the woman I'd picked up at the bar last night, and who was now sleeping naked in my bed.

I ran my finger down her spine. She stirred.

"Mmmm, good morning."
"Morning sleepyhead. Do you want some breakfast?"
"Yeah. Hmmm, last night was nice."
"It was. I'd like to do some more nice things, but I have to run to the office."
"Are you sure?" She smiled deviously.
"Well . . . we could jump in the shower together, you know, to save water."
"Of course, to save water."

In the shower, I stood behind Mandy and slid my hands over her body. She unscrewed the top to the liquid soap and poured it down her back, then pressed against me. I bent her forward until her hands rested against the wall. She gasped as I entered her.

"Ooooh," she moaned. I moved her hand towards her stomach.

"Play with yourself while I fuck you." I said. "Play with your clit."
She did as told. Soon she was breathing harder and thrusting back into me.
"Cum for me!" I grabbed her hair and pulled. "Cum!"
"Oh, oh, ohhhhhhhh" she moaned as she came. I pumped her a few more times before pulling out. She sank to her knees and took me in her mouth, licking and sucking until I exploded.

All clean, I left for the office to meet my new advisees.

When a student transfers to Clareville, they're assigned a temporary advisor within their major. After a semester, the student then chooses whether to remain with that advisor or switch to someone else in the department. This year there were 12 transfers, which meant everyone had two new students. Mine were Bill Moreno and Bryn Daniels.

We had exchanged a few emails, and I'd been impressed by both of them. Bill came from a poor background and had transferred out of a community college. Bryn didn't give away her background in our correspondence. She was very direct and prompt with her replies, though, which I liked.

At the office I gave a quick hello to Amy, the psychology department's shared secretary. I'd helped Amy's son, Ryan, when he'd gotten into trouble for partying too much and Amy has been overly grateful ever since. Honestly, I just listened to the kid and explained how to get by while still having a good time. To hear Amy tell it, though, I saved his life. The upside was that any request I made went to the top of her list.

The downside is that I had to listen to Amy's excruciatingly long updates about Ryan.

Fortunately, Bill was waiting for me outside my office when I got there, so I sped by Amy with a quick hello and shook hands with Bill. He had a quick smile and I liked him instantly. We talked about his goals and his background. He was the first member of his family to go to college. He'd worked extremely hard in community college and described the day he received his scholarship to Clareville as one of the happiest of his life. He had a midwestern earnestness about him. He would make good, I was sure. And I would do what I could to help him.

I'd help Bryn, too, but something told me she wouldn't need it. She'd already won the genetic lottery: she was five-feet nine and gorgeous, with wavy brown hair down to her mid-back, blue eyes and breasts that defied gravity. She looked like a model for very expensive perfume. Watching her walk towards me, I got the impression that she came from extreme wealth. I can't say exactly why; she just seemed like she had spent a lot of time on horses when she was young.

I know how to handle beautiful women, which is to treat them like normal people. They deal with so many creepy guys fawning over their every move and laughing too hard at their jokes. A beautiful woman, like all women, wants real conversation, not some guy kissing her ass or – worse – putting her down to try to show he's higher status than she is. Just be normal. We talked, and as Bryn realized that I wasn't some slimeball professor who was going to stare at her tits all the time, she relaxed and let more of her personality come out. She was extremely bright, with a dark sense of humor similar to my own. We got along well.

Classes started. It seemed like a promising crop. I was teaching an intro to psychology lecture and an upper level social psychology seminar, the latter based on motivation.

Bryn was in my seminar, and she distinguished herself early with her insight about subconscious triggers. She seemed to know a lot about getting people to respond to cues without them realizing it. Bill was bright as well. But where Bill's intelligence and charisma made other students like him, Bryn’s intimidated people. Maybe it was her tone, which had a subtle arrogance. Or maybe people just thought it unfair that someone so gorgeous was also smart and confident. I got a kick out of her, though, and often, after she said something particularly intimidating, I saw just the slightest grin on her face. She knew exactly how she came across to other students, and she liked it.

I saw Mandy a bunch of times. It was fun. The sex was great, but the relationship wasn't going anywhere and I was starting to feel restless. I'm not in a hurry to give away my freedom, and while she was nice, I just wasn't ready to be tied down. It reminded me of a cartoon someone had emailed me in which a man explained to a woman, "this has been great, but I'd like to go back to doing whatever I want all the time." That's pretty much how I felt.

We went out for dinner and drinks at the Elbo Room, the bar and restaurant closest to my house and my favorite place to drink. As we entered the restaurant, we ran into Bryn with a date. He looked familiar.

"Dr. Clark, what a nice surprise." She turned to Mandy, "I'm Bryn, one of Taylor's advisees."
Mandy gave Bryn a somewhat cold hello, which Bryn either didn't notice or ignored. My guess was the latter.
"This is Jim." She turned to her date, who I then recognized as a wide receiver on our school's football team. He stood silently next to her. "Jim, say hello."
"Hi," he said.
"Go get us a table," Bryn addressed him like a servant.
He looked at her for just a moment, deciding whether he deserved better, then did as told.
"Great seeing you, Dr. Clark. Nice to meet you, Mandy." And with that she took off.
"She seems like a real bitch," Mandy said.
"She's actually very nice." But I had to agree, she did seem bitchy just then.

Later that dinner, Mandy talked about becoming more serious, and I had to let her down gently. She wasn't happy about it and ended up storming out of the restaurant. I knew she wanted me to run after her, but I wasn't about to turn the end of a month-long fling into some opera, so I paid my bill and went to the bar for a Black Label scotch. I was half-way through it when I felt someone nudge my arm.

"Howdy, stranger."
It was Bryn. When I'd seen her entering the restaurant, she had been wearing a light sweater. But she'd removed it during dinner to reveal a low-cut dress that showed off her cleavage. It was difficult not to stare, but I didn't. I gave myself a mental pat on the back for that.
"Where's Jim?"
"I sent him home. Where's Mandy?"
"She left. She has an early morning tomorrow and had to get home."

She studied me for a moment, and I knew she was using the secret power that females have to know when you're lying. But she didn't push further.

"Buy a poor student a drink?"
"I could be wrong, Bryn, but I don't think you're poor."
"No, you're not wrong. But just because someone's parents have money doesn't mean they give it to her."
"True. But are you even 21?"
Instead of answering, she reached into her purse and tossed her driver's license on the bar in front of me. I picked it up. Of course it was a flattering picture. She was exactly the kind of girl to have a hot driver's license picture. Mine made me look like I had died several days prior and was starting to decompose. I read her birthdate: she was 24.

"I took some years off between high school and college to work."
I nodded. I felt a little bad for my earlier impression of her as a spoiled kid.
"My parents were big on me learning responsibility. They said they'd pay for college and a place to live. But books, food and spending money were up to me. So I worked to save up."
"Funny thing, my parents were the same way."
We sat in the shared connection for a moment before I caught the bartender's attention.
"My friend here will have . . ."
"Johnnie Walker Black, neat."
"You have good taste for someone so young." I lifted my glass and the bartender filled mine up as well. I looked at Bryn and saw the corners of her mouth go up.
"Funny," she said, "I had you pegged as the Shirley Temple type."

"The bartender cut me off. I get a little crazy when I drink Shirley Temples."
It was a dumb joke, but she laughed anyway. I lifted my glass:
"Cheers,"
"To the start of a beautiful friendship," she said, clinking my glass with hers.

A week later, I was sitting in my office on a Friday afternoon. My classes were going well and I was reading through my advanced students' theses' proposals. My social psych seminars were year-long courses, and each student would complete an independent research project about motivation. Students had to turn in the first draft of their project proposals by this afternoon, and every one, save Bryn, had done so. I wasn't surprised when she showed up at my office. She knocked and then entered without waiting for my reply.

"Dr. Clark."
"Bryn, come on in."
She sat and stared at me for a moment without speaking. I stared back.
“How's Mandy?"
"We're not seeing each other anymore."
"Why?"
"Several reasons." I didn't feel like talking about it with her.
"Pity," she said, but she didn't mean it.
"Sure."
"I broke up with Jim, too."
I nodded
She looked at me and smiled, "also for several reasons."
I smiled back, Bryn's smile was contagious, "pity."
She held my gaze without speaking for a few seconds, "is it?"

It was time to shift gears.
“You’re here to discuss your thesis."
"You're very perceptive, Taylor. What would you like to know?"
"For starters, what is it?"
"You'll like it. It's about manipulation. It's my belief that people subconsciously give clues to exactly what's needed to control them. If you ask the right questions and elicit the right emotions, you can discover how to pull anyone’s strings, and you can get them to do things they would normally never do, all the while thinking you're doing them a favor."
"Interesting. And unethical. What would you like to do instead?"
"Don't worry. I'll use words like "drive" and "motivation" and talk about how we can motivate inner city kids to want to succeed in schools. I'll also throw in some talk about discipline and the need for hard work, and people on both sides of the aisle will love it."
"You'll manipulate people into liking your study on manipulation. How meta."
She leaned forward. Bryn had a number of different smiles at her disposal, and she unleashed her mischievous one. I think she wanted me to look at her breasts. I stared at her eyes.
"I think you like my idea."
"Maybe. But find a different way to describe it."

I had a feeling Bryn would end up ruling the world, or at least finding a way to make a lot of people do what she wanted. Truth be told, she had that ability already, if Jim was any indication.

"If I do allow you to go forward with this idea, what poor soul is going to be your subject?"
"He's around."

"I feel bad for him."
"Why? In the end he'll thank me."

As she said it, she smiled, and I got the impression she was imagining something sexual and deviant. I pictured her then in just a bra and panties, standing over an indistinct man who was kneeling at her feet.

"Taylor?"

I came back to the present and hastily collected some papers on my desk for no good reason.

"Well, Bryn, I've got some work to do, why don't we schedule-"
"How about a ride home?"
"What?"
"I'm going home, and I thought you were, too, and we live near each other, so how about a ride?"
"How do you know where I live?"
"I saw you jogging the other day."
She started to gather her books as if I'd already said yes, which irritated me. I was getting too friendly with Bryn, and she was getting way too familiar with me.

I didn't get up. Bryn looked to the right, and in what was obviously her go-to move, arched her back and ran both hands through her hair, gathering it behind her head before letting fall. It lifted and highlighted her breasts in devastating fashion.
I met her eyes.
"Are we going?"
"No."
"No?"
"No."
"Why not?"

I wondered if this were the first time anyone had ever said no to Bryn. She was acting like it.
"I have more work to do. I'm going to do it here."
She stared at me, waiting for me to give in, as I'm sure everyone else in her life had. But I wasn't some love-struck classmate or desperate professor. I was her advisor and she was my student, and I wasn't giving her a ride.
"See you tomorrow, Bryn."

I felt good after this exchange. It was important with young, beautiful women to stand your ground and control the situation.

Five days later, I gave her a ride. She came into my office to discuss her reworked thesis proposal. She had a large box with her, some package that had been delivered to the school post office instead of her apartment. In addition, she had listened to my criticism of her proposal and made the necessary changes to make it at least not an ethical disaster. When we were finished talking, she started collecting her things. She lifted the box, which was clearly heavy. I thought about what I would have done if Bryn were just a normal-looking girl. I would have offered her a ride.

"Bryn, I'll give you a ride home."
"Are you sure?"
"C'mon, before I change my mind."

Bryn followed me to my pride and joy, my midnight blue Mustang convertible. She laughed when she realized which car was mine.

"You know what a psychologist would say about a man who drives a sports car, right Dr. Clark?"

"I know a psychology student would say 'awesome car, Dr. Clark!' . . . unless she'd rather walk."
"Awesome car Dr. Clark!"
"Thatta girl."

We got in, and she met my gaze and held it, not smiling but not frowning either. I stared back. Bryn liked to make people uncomfortable. I'd seen it in class and noticed it every so often in our conversations. She would hold eye-contact without smiling, trying to see if the other person would look away. It struck me as rooted in insecurity, her need to be dominant all the time. It was hard to imagine Bryn as insecure, but maybe she'd had to wear headgear as a kid.

The drive to her place would have taken ten minutes if there hadn't been traffic, but there was traffic. And so we crawled along, making small talk. Turns out she hadn't had to wear headgear when she was younger. Her phone rang, and when she answered, her tone was harsh and stern, like with Jim at the restaurant.

"What is it, Marty? . . . No . . . what did I tell you? . . . So why do I have to tell you again? . . . . Do it now, then come over in an hour and we'll deal with this."

Embarrassingly, I was turned on by the way she bossed around Marty. And to make it worse, it was almost impossible not to stare at her cleavage as she talked. For some reason it had magnetic qualities today. Fortunately my pants hid my erection. When she hung up, I tried to make light of the call.

"Good friend?"

She turned to me sharply. "Why were you listening to my phone call?"

For a moment I felt like a school kid who'd forgotten his homework. I almost apologized before I remembered that I was a professor and she was my student.

"I can't not hear you talk on the phone when we're in a car together. My ears don't turn off."

She held my gaze and I felt my cock stir.

"Fair enough," she said, and turned her gaze back towards the road.

We drove for a while in silence.

"I'm sorry. I shouldn't have snapped at you. I'm just fed up with Marty and tired of hearing him whine. College boys can't follow even the simplest directions."

I wondered what those directions were but didn't ask. What she did and thought on her own time was her business. I just felt sorry for Marty. Poor sap.

She lived on the ground floor of a very nice colonial house on the outskirts of town, about a five-minute walk from my house. She said that she rented the apartment from a nice, older couple who charged low rent in exchange for her helping them with some chores. Hearing that made me like Bryn even more.

Most students lived closer to campus and the center of town, but it didn't surprise me that she wanted to live here. Walking through town late on a Friday or Saturday meant running into packs of drunken frat boys, and I didn't imagine Bryn having the patience for that. I pulled over in front. She gathered up the box from the backseat, along with her shoulder bag and purse and turned to me:

"Thanks for the ride, Taylor. I'd invite you in for a drink, but Marty's coming over. It'll have to wait."

Then, her gaze fell to my crotch. She couldn't know that I had an erection, could she? She smiled and walked away. At home, I gathered my lube from under the bed and squeezed a generous helping in my palm.

When I was ten, my parents took a two-week vacation to Europe and left me with a babysitter from the local college named Natalie. She was a heavy-set, serious woman who I immediately decided was beneath me. With all the bravado of a dumb pre-teen, I told her that I didn't need some fat girl telling me what to do. She studied me for a moment, then grabbed my arm and twisted it behind my back. She must have studied some type of martial art, because my arm felt like it was going to snap. She marched me to my bedroom and pushed me forward over my bed.

"Do you want me to break your arm?" She spoke through clenched teeth.
"No! No!!" I was panicking: the pain was intense.
"Then don't move." She reached around and undid the button to my pants, then yanked them down around my ankles, followed by my underwear. She sat on the bed and pulled me over her knee. Shamefully, I started to cry, even before the first spanks fell.
"You – whap, whap – are going to listen to me – whap, whap, whap – and do what I say – whap – when I say – whap – how I say – whap, whap, whap – or I will put you over my knee every day – whap, whap, whap!

I hadn't struggled; I just lay there sobbing and shaking as she rained down the blows. I lost count, but it was over fifty. When I was done, she made me stand in front of her and apologize, then go stand in the corner with my pants and underwear still around my ankles. After what seemed like forever, she called me back to stand in front of her. My cheeks were still red from crying. I stared at her feet, but she grabbed my chin and lifted my gaze to meet hers.

"Am I going to have any more trouble?"
"No."
"No what?"
"No Natalie."
"That's better. Are you going to be a good boy?"
"Yes, Natalie."
"Good. Now go back to the corner for another ten minutes. I'll let you know when you can come out."

For the next two weeks I did everything she asked: cleaning the house from top to bottom, running errands for her, even doing her laundry. I didn't think of it as sexual at the time, but I've masturbated to it countless times. Sometimes I take it farther, where Natalie jacks me off. Other times I pop before she's even done spanking me.

As a psychologist, I know it's probably not the healthiest of masturbation choices, but it's not like I pay women to beat me or am in some sick, co-dependent relationship, so I don't see any harm to it. And I cum like a rocket.

Listening to Bryn browbeat Marty made me want to revisit that episode from my past, so I lay on my bed and pictured standing in front of Natalie post spanking, imagining her firmly taking my cock in her hand and stroking it.

"Are you going to be a good boy?"

I exploded.

Chapter 2

The next month went by quickly. I appeared on a cable news program to talk about a religious cult in Idaho. I should have had the first chapter of my book written, but I couldn’t find the motivation. My classes were going well. Bryn came to talk with me during office hours regularly, and we grew close. I felt like she was growing attached to me, and it was my responsibility to keep her at arm's length.

There were a couple episodes that made me wary of her, too. The first was at the Elbo Room, which is my main spot for picking up women. It's pretty much student-free, which is important for obvious reasons. Bryn started hanging out there, and I felt like she was invading my space. I didn't want one of my students around when I hit on women.

One night I spotted Bryn at the bar. She hadn't seen me, so I watched as a man approached and tried to talk with her. She wasn't having it. She turned away and ignored him, and he, like a true asshole, grabbed her arm. I stood up, ready to sprint over and pound his face in, but Bryn apparently didn't need my help. She reached down and grabbed his crotch as she leant forward and whispered in his ear. Whatever she said, it worked, because his cocky demeanor disappeared and he beat it out of there. I felt I should go over and ask if she were ok, but the look on her face was cruel and mocking, and something told me she had enjoyed the confrontation.

Three days later, I was talking with Bill, my student advisee. He and Bryn were working on a project together, and I asked him how it was going.
"It's going well. Bryn has strong opinions."

I laughed. "I know."
"It could be worse, though, I could be dating her."
That remark caught me short.
"Why do you say that?"
"She uses guys. She gets them doing whatever she wants and then she dumps them. She's really hot, so we used to ask Jim what she was like in bed, but he wouldn't tell us. He just said she was fucked up. I think she sleeps with a lot of dudes."

Later that day, as I was going over some notes for my paper in my office, I heard the door open and then close. Bryn came and sat across from my desk.

"Bryn, you have to knock before you come in my office." I went back to my notes.
"Sorry. I'd like some help on my paper."

She said "sorry" so casually and meaninglessly that it bothered me. People just did whatever Bryn wanted, whenever she wanted it. That bothered me.
"Bryn, go outside and knock on my door, then you can come in and I'll help you."
"Are you joking?"
"No."
"What are you, twelve?!"
I looked up at her. Who did she think she was talking to?
"Now you have to leave."
"Oh my God! That's so stupid!"
"Goodbye Bryn."

Bryn kept her face neutral. She nodded slowly, then picked up her bag and left.

I had acted like an asshole, but she deserved it. And my guess was she'd realize that and apologize. Sure enough, the next day around 3pm I got the following email.

> *Dr. Clark,*
> *I'm sorry I was so rude yesterday. I understand that it's your office and will knock when I come by in the future.*
> *Best,*
> *Bryn*

Now that I'd gotten her apology I felt better. Our relationship had been getting too informal again, but now I'd reestablished myself as in control. I emailed her back.

> *Bryn,*
> *Don't worry about the other day. What was your question on your research paper? I'd be happy to talk to you about it.*
> *Best,*
> *Dr. Clark*

A few minutes later:

> *Dr. Clark,*
> *I'm at The Elbo Room having a drink. Why don't you join me and we'll talk about psychology over a scotch?*
> *Bryn*

This wasn't a good idea, and I needed to work on my book, but a scotch sounded good right then. She was at a corner table, working on her laptop with a glass of scotch in front of her. Since she didn't see me, I took a moment to admire her from the doorway. She had a worldliness about her that was rare for a 24 year-old. And she radiated sexuality. I realized I was treading dangerous ground meeting her like this, but I trusted my own self-control. I'd had beautiful students before, and more than one of them had made it very clear they were mine for the taking. But I always kept control of myself. I was good at it. The bar was empty except for the bartender and waiter chatting at the end of the bar. Bryn didn't see me approaching.

"Excuse me, can I join you? There aren't any other open seats."
She looked up at me and smiled her kind smile, then closed her computer.
"Not a bad line."
"It's better than not bad."
"I've heard better."
I sat down.
"What's your question about your project?"
"Let's get you a drink first." She nodded to the waiter and he hustled over.
"The esteemed professor here will have a double scotch, neat. Johnnie Walker Black."
The waiter looked at me. I shrugged.
"She's the boss."
We talked for a while about her project and I gave her ways to refine her approach and make it something she might eventually publish. She was appreciative and insisted on buying me another scotch, which I shouldn't have drunk but did anyway. Bryn closed her computer and shifted the conversation to more personal topics.
"So what happened with Mandy? She seemed . . . interesting."
"You didn't like her."
"I did."
"No, Bryn, you didn't."

She leaned back in her chair and folded her arms over her chest.
"Fine. She seemed like a bitch. I didn't think I gave that away."
"I'm a good read of people."
"Clearly."
"What happened to Tim?"
"Jim."
"What happened to Jim?"
She made dismissive gesture with her hand. "Jim's a boy."
"Couldn't handle you?"

She met my eyes without smiling.

"No."

This wasn't smart. Two scotches in, I was very attracted to my student across the table, and I knew she was attracted to me. She cocked her head to one side and kept eye contact.

No. Time to leave. She was beautiful, but there were other beautiful women who wouldn't leave me begging them to keep our affair quiet. My job at Clareville was the most important thing in my life, and an affair with a student would jeopardize my tenure.

"I have to go."
"What?"
"I have some work to do. Sorry." I stood up too quickly and lost my balance. I took an awkward step forward, stepping on her foot.
Bryn looked at me with narrowed eyes and pursed lips. She wasn't used to not getting her way, especially with

men in bars. When I held my ground, her face softened, and she looked down at her feet.

"I understand. You're right. You should go. But promise me you're not driving."
"Fine."
"Where's your car?"
"Outside."
"C'mon, I'll drive you home. We live right next to each other, practically."
"I can drive."
"You can't even stand up without falling over!"
"Bryn, I'm fine."
"Dr. Clark, my friend got hit by a drunk driver and nearly died. I'm not letting you drive."

I let her drive me home. She wasn't talkative in the car, and neither was I. It felt like a date that had lasted an hour too long. She pulled up in front of my house.
"I'm taking your car home."
"What?!"
"You can pick it up tomorrow. You were going to have to pick it up from the bar, anyway. And I'm not walking home." She fixed me with an icy look. "Are you going to apologize for stomping on my foot."
"I'm sorry."
"You're sorry for what?"
I reacted without thinking. Maybe it was the liquor. "I'm sorry for stepping on your foot."
"Good. Now go."

Something about her bitchiness went right to my groin. She was dismissing me and taking my car, and instead of being angry or stopping her, I was completely turned on. Inside, I went right to my bedroom and grabbed the lube. I pictured Natalie pulling me over her lap and

spanking me, but I kept seeing Bryn's face. It was one of my superstitions never to masturbate about a student, but every time I pictured myself with Natalie, Bryn's image would take over. I pictured her straddling me on the bed, looking down at me with a haughty expression:
"I knew you couldn't resist me."
I was quickly nearing orgasm when the phone rang. I ignored it and went back to imaginary Bryn riding me. I came like a freight train.

The next day I walked to Bryn's place and knocked on her door. She opened looking way more cheerful than I felt. If she resented me for not falling prey to her charms the day before, she wasn't letting it show.

"Hold on for a second. I'll get your keys and we can go in together. I just need to grab something."
I should have told her I was in a hurry and didn't have time to wait around. Instead, I waited outside for what seemed like a long time. I was in hurry, and here I was waiting for a student because I was dumb enough to let her take my car. When she finally came outside I was in a foul mood. She didn't apologize of course; she just tossed me my keys.
"Why didn't you pick up when I called last night?"
"When did you call?"
"Not long after I dropped you off. What were you doing?"
"I don't remember."
"Yes you do."

When I looked at her she was smiling as if she knew exactly what I'd been doing. I scowled.

"I'm just joking. God! You're making me think you were up to no good, Dr. Clark."

"Bryn, what do want?!" My voice came out sharper than I'd wanted. "I'm giving you a ride to school, just be grateful and stop acting like doing you favors is my main mission in life."
"I don't. I was just kidding!"
"Well stop it. I'm your professor, Bryn, not your friend."
She was silent for a moment.
"Fine, sorry. God."

We drove in silence the rest of the way. Bryn stared out the window. When we pulled into the school, she turned, and I saw her eyes were wet.

"You were cruel to me at school the other day. I know, I should have knocked, but you went out of your way to humiliate me. I tried to make a peace offering to you and bought you drinks, and then you acted weird and tried to run away, like I was going to attack you." She sniffled, and tears fell down her cheeks. "I give you a ride home so you don't get arrested for drunk driving, and instead of being thankful, you act like I'm trying to take advantage of you"
She wiped her face.
“I don't have any real friends at this school, Dr. Clark. The boys look at me like a sex toy, and the girls are all catty and jealous. All I want is to be treated like a real person, and you’re the only one who did that. I thought you were someone I could talk to, and I don't know why you suddenly seem to hate me."

She ended her speech as I parked. She didn't wait for a response. She just got out of the car, slammed the door and walked away.

I felt terrible. She was right. What had she done to deserve how I'd treated her? She hadn't been hitting on me; I'd just been worried that *I'd* make a move on her. And at the office the other day: that was stupid. I was treating her differently because she was beautiful. And for all her beauty and sophistication, she was still just a kid. She deserved better than that.

I'd hoped she would come to office hours that day so I could apologize to her, but she didn't show. She didn't come the next day, either. Then, to make matters worse, she didn't come to class. I kept looking at the door, hoping she'd come in late. I was disappointed beyond reason. Was she punishing me?

That night I felt restless, so I went to the gym and worked out. I had to get Bryn off my mind. I was acting like a stupid teenager. It was a good thing she wasn't coming by anymore. My feelings towards her were way out of line and getting in the way of my common sense.

So of course, the next day, Bryn came to my office just as office hours were ending and I was packing up to go. I couldn't help but smile when she walked in.

"Howdy stranger."
"Hi Dr. Clark." Her voice was formal.
"Bryn, about the other day. I'm sorry. I was a jerk. Will you accept my apology?"
She looked at me for a moment.
"Fine."

She was obviously still hurt.
"Let's talk about your project, Bryn. I was thinking about it last night and there are some articles I think would really help you."

"Ok, but let's do it on the ride home."

I hadn't offered her a ride, but I was leaving, and I did owe her one.

"So about your thesis" I said in the car. "Do you have a victim, I mean subject?"
"I have a subject, yes, and I think he'll be very good for this project. I'm quickly learning how to, um, motivate him."
"Is it Marty?"
"You're very smart, Dr. Clark."
"I feel bad for him," I lied. "Does he know what you're up to?"
"He thinks he's too smart to be controlled by little ol' me." I smiled at that. It was typical male stupidity that would get Marty to practically enslave himself to Bryn.
"Poor guy. You won't completely ruin him, will you?"
"Maybe, but he'll be better off under my control."

I felt my penis stir. This woman! We pulled up outside her place.

"Well, have a good night, Bryn."
"Wait, Dr. Clark, I have a favor to ask of you."
"What?"
"I know this is a lot, and I understand if the answer is no, but they're doing repair work on the water line here and there's no running water. The couple that owns the house are really sweet, but they're not good at getting things fixed. Can I use your shower?"

This sounded like a very bad idea. It felt like she was testing me, seeing how sorry I was. I wasn't sure I was *that* sorry.

"Please, Dr. Clark. I have a date tonight and I want to look good for it."

There didn't seem to be any way out of this one.
“Sure, Bryn. Come on over."

She ran inside for a moment to get some clothes to change into, and we drove to my place. I had hoped Bryn would take a quick shower and leave, but she was intent on checking out my apartment, looking at my photos and commenting on my lack of decorating skills. Finally, I steered her to the upstairs bathroom and gave her a towel. She showered as I went downstairs to the kitchen.

I thought about doing some work, but my computer was upstairs in my office, and I didn't want to be anywhere near the bathroom when she was showering. Bryn took a long time, which didn't surprise me. She finally came downstairs wearing a forest-green, tight, low-cut dress and high heels. She looked amazing, and for a moment I was speechless.

"How do I look?"
"You look good."
"Good?"
"Yes, good . . . it's a compliment."

She gave me her pout.
"Dr. Clark, I don't know if you've noticed this about women, but we like our compliments with a little more gusto."
"Good doesn't count as full of gusto?"
"It does not."

"Interesting." I pretended to think about that. "I see your point. Ask me again how you look. I promise I'll do better this time."

She studied me for a moment to see if I was full of shit. "How do I look?"
I paused.
"You look good." She let go with a shout and playfully punched me in the arm. We both laughed, and I felt the last bit of tension from our fight give way. It was nice to be on good terms with her again.

"You're a bad boy, Dr. Clark. One of these days you're going to get punished."
I wasn't looking at her when she said it, which was a good thing, because the look on my face might have given me away. It was like she hit a switch: I was completely turned on.

"C'mon Dr. Clark. I need a ride home."
"What?! Bryn, you live three minutes away."
"Mr. Clark, look at these heels. Have you ever walked around in high heels?"
"Yes, Bryn, all the time." I waited for her to smile. She didn't. "Fine, let's go."

When we got to her place, she said goodbye and patted my cheek in either a friendly or a condescending way, I couldn't tell which. I didn't care. I sped back home to my bedroom and grabbed the lube. I brought myself close to cumming and then backed away, then close to cumming and backed away again. Finally, on the third time I let myself explode, shooting cum all over my chest. I sat there panting. It was then that I realized Bryn hadn't thanked me for the ride or for letting her use my shower.

Chapter 3

I didn't see Bryn for a few days after that. But it was as if she had cast a spell on me. On Thursday night, I felt restless, so I went to the gym and worked out. But half an hour after coming home, I was restless again, so I masturbated. This time I grabbed the towel she had used and held it to my face as I masturbated. Jesus! I needed to get a grip on myself.

On Friday afternoon, Bryn sauntered into my office, again not knocking. She looked a little different, but I couldn't say why. She was dressed well, but she dressed well normally. She seemed more confident than usual, which is saying something about a girl who always looks confident. That said, she'd once again come in without knocking.

"Bryn, do I really have to beg you to knock?"
"Hmm, I like that image, you begging me."

She walked towards my desk slowly, staring me in the eyes the whole time.

"I have something to show you."

"Bryn, I don't really have time."
"You need to see this."
"It can wait."

She came around my desk and stood close to me.

"Taylor, I don't think it can."

There was something about her self-assuredness that triggered alarm bells. Even before she leaned in and whispered in my ear, I knew something was wrong.

"I know what you did with my towel."

For a second I didn't know what she meant. Towel? What towel? But – how could she know what I did with her towel?

"Get your things. We're leaving." Bryn's voice was hard. It was the voice she had used in the car with Marty.

I tried to get Bryn to talk in the car, but she wouldn't. When we got to her place, she didn't wait for me, just got out of the car, said, "follow me," and walked inside.

Her place was beautiful. I don't know who decorated it, the older couple or her, but whoever it was had expensive taste and the money to indulge it. She took me into a large living room with modern, leather furniture and a plush rug. She pointed to the sofa facing a large television.

"Sit."

I thought about walking out. What could she possibly have on me? But how did she know about the towel? She was bluffing. But in my chest I knew that she was not the kind of girl who bluffed. I sat down on the couch as she disappeared upstairs.

I'm not sure how long I waited. About ten times I thought about leaving, but something kept me there. I knew Bryn admired me, so she wouldn't do anything to hurt our relationship or my standing at the college. So what was I doing here? She finally came downstairs carrying her computer. She hooked it up to the television.

She faced me and smiled. It was the smile of an animal about to eat a smaller and weaker animal. She pressed play on the computer.

My mouth fell open and I felt like I was going to vomit. There on the screen was me on my bed masturbating. I looked like a complete pervert and possibly insane. I watched as I brought myself closer to the edge several times before finally ejaculating.

"Hold on, this next one's even better."

It was, of course, me holding the towel up to my face as I jerked off. Oh Christ, what was happening? Bryn looked at me with hurt and anger.

"You let me use your shower, and then you masturbate with my towel! What kind of sicko are you? How am I supposed to feel safe around you?!"

I started to stammer an apology.

"Don't! I can't believe you did this to me! I trusted you!"

Then it hit me.

"Bryn, how did get this video?"
"Never mind that!"
"Bryn, did you install a camera in my bedroom? You did it after you showered, didn't you?"

She stared at me. Slowly, her wounded expression changed into a wide grin.

"Before the shower, actually."
"Ok, you have videos of me masturbating and looking like an idiot. So now you're going to blackmail me?!"
My temper was rising. I stood up and took a step in her direction.
"Wait, Taylor, there's more. Look."

She pulled up her email. Oddly, there was one from me from the other day. I didn't remember emailing her. I hadn't.
"You sent me some disturbing fetish videos, Here, look."

Thinking of you, bitch!

I stopped and stared at her, confused. She looked at me like I was a stupid child. I finally got it.

"You got on my computer and sent those to yourself."
She smiled. This had just gone from bad to dangerous. She showed me another email. I didn't bother reading what "I" had written her. Posting videos of me online would embarrass me, but I would live. This though, the appearance that I sent them to a student, that would get me fired and blacklisted.

I breathed deeply to control my myself. I stared at her. It was her move. She took a big breath in and exhaled.

"Let me explain what's going to happen. You will now choose between two options. Option one is you leave. However, you should know that your video has already been uploaded to eleven different porn sites, including a new website I made in your honor, TaylorClark.com, that will show up first in any search of your name. That site will go live in two hours unless I log in to each of them and remove your videos. In addition, the emails you sent me, along with video attachments, will be sent to every single student and teacher on campus, along with a letter from me explaining your constant harassment. That's option one."

"And option two?"

"Option two is you become my slave."

I looked at her. She was serious.
"What does being your slave entail?"

She walked up to me and patted my cheek with her hand, this time it was clearly condescending.

"Uh-uh. You'll find out if you choose option two. But I want to show you something else, just in case you're thinking of doing something violent."

She walked back to her computer and brought up her email. She then opened two more emails from my account. The first read:

> *Bryn,*
> *I know you're a slut and want me. I can see it in your eyes, so don't ever turn me down again! If you want to pass my class, understand that I get what I want.*
> *-T*

The second was just as ridiculous, though this time even more threatening:

Bryn,
You fucking bitch! This is your last warning. Don't get me angry. Other bitches have learned that lesson the hard way.
-T

I hadn't sent those emails to Bryn, of course. But it sure looked I did.

"Those are a nice touch, Bryn."
"I thought you'd like them. See how you imply that you've done it before? Those two emails, along with a note saying how worried I am about your increasingly menacing advances towards poor, defenseless me, also go out to the administration and the local police, unless of course you agree to option two. And – I think you'll like this – I sent all of this to a friend, and if anything happens to me, she'll send them to the police."

I wanted to choke her, but I couldn't. I closed my eyes. She had me.

"Bryn, you'd really do this to me?"
"Yes." She spoke plainly. "I would."
"Why? I've helped you!"
"Because I want you as my slave. You're sexy, and sweet in a rough kind of way. All the boys at school are morons, Taylor, but not you. You're smart and fun to be around. I want you as my lover, and this is what I do with my lovers."

"This isn't normal, Bryn. You're fucked up!"

"And masturbating with a used towel is? Spare me the judgment." She waited for me to respond, but I didn't. "I don't want a boring relationship where we argue about who takes out the trash and cleans the toilet. And I don't want to read Cosmo for ways I can get you to start satisfying me in bed. I want a slave who worships me, who fears me, who I can tie up and punish and humiliate whenever I want. Think about it Taylor: you naked and kneeling before me, cleaning my feet with your tongue." She breathed in deeply while staring at me. "I'm getting wet just thinking about it."

She walked over and took my head in her hands. She aimed my vision at her chest.

"I know how hard you try not to stare at my breasts. It's really touching. Do you really think I can't tell? You're like a puppy when you stare at me. And don't pretend like you don't want to serve me. You're practically my slave already. Think about it: you've done everything I've ever asked you to do, even driving me four blocks home so I wouldn't have to walk in my heels. And I saw how hard you got in the car when I yelled at Marty. You want to be my slave. The sooner you admit it the better."

She stood up and walked across the room.

"It was me all along: the guy you'd manipulate, who you'd ruin?"

"Of course, but like I said, you'll learn to love it. Now get down on your knees and crawl to me. Plant a kiss on each of my feet, and let me hear you say it."

I couldn't move. I quickly went through all of our interactions in my mind and saw how expertly Bryn had played me. I wondered how much of what she said was real. I tried to think of something, anything I could do.

"What do you want, Bryn? Do you want money? Do you want my car?"
"Don't be stupid. Look around Dr. Clark. Does it look like I need money?"

It didn't.

"Time's running out, Taylor. Those videos go out soon. Think about what that would mean for you."

I sank to my knees and crawled to her. Everything seemed to be moving very fast. I kissed her left foot, then her right.

"I choose option two. I agree to be your slave."

Chapter 4

"Lift your head up, my slave." Bryn softly held my cheeks and brought her lips to mine, kissing me slowly. Despite all she was doing to me, or maybe because of it, it was one of best kisses I'd ever had. Bryn seemed to read my thoughts.

"See pet. It can be fun and romantic for you, too. Now, I'm going to go downstairs for some supplies. When I come back I want you naked and kneeling with your forehead on the ground, hands behind your back. Clear?"

I nodded. She gave me her sweet smile and touched my nose with her finger. Before she left, she put the video of me masturbating back on the television. I stared at the floor as her footsteps receded down the hall and downstairs. What was I doing? What could I do? Should I run and hope that she was bluffing? Too risky. This video playing in front of me was really bad. And those emails were a brilliant touch. Jesus. She could ruin me – really ruin me. I'd never get hired anywhere again. All my hard work, gone! No, running was not an option, and neither was violence. I would go along with her plan for now. My guess is she wanted kinky sex and some fun with a man she admired. It would make for an interesting few weeks, but then, hopefully, she would move on to her next victim. The video of me finished, then started again: she'd set it to loop.

I took off my clothes and folded them. Then I got back on my knees and lowered my head to the floor. It was uncomfortable. My knees hurt, and keeping my head on the floor without the support of my hands forced me forward, putting weight onto my forehead.

I waited. I don't know how much time went by: Ten minutes? Twenty? What was taking so long?

Finally I heard the click of heels coming up the stairs, then down the hallway and into the room behind me. She took one wrist and placed a handcuff around it, closing it with a *click.* Then she cuffed my other wrist. She applied another set of cuffs to my ankles. If I'd had any plans about running, they were now ruined.

"Up, pet. On your knees."

I pushed myself up. Oh my God! Bryn had changed clothes. She was wearing 4-inch spiked heels, fishnet stockings and a leather mini skirt. On top she wore a black leather corset. She had put on darker eye-liner and more lipstick. She had always looked sexy, now she looked absolutely breathtaking.

"Oh my God!"

She placed her index finger over my lips. "Shh, slave. No speaking except to answer questions. Nod that you understand." I nodded. "Good, now I'm going to present to you something very special. It's your collar. It signifies that you're my slave and I'm your master. When you're wearing it you're to address me as Master. So if I say, "do you accept my collar?" You reply "Yes Master." Understood?" Behind her on the television, I was climaxing.

"Yes Master."

"Good. I'll go over the rules with you downstairs. But know that not addressing me by my title is a serious no-no."

She held my leather collar in front of me. It was simple: black, about an inch and a half wide. Hanging down from the center was a medal that read "T."

"I had this collar made for you two months ago." She held my chin in her hand. "Now little one, do you accept my collar?"

This was ridiculous. Why the farce? I wasn't accepting anything, and we both knew it. Still, I knew I had to go along with it.

"Yes, Master."
"Good boy." She fastened the collar around my neck. She stared at my cock for a moment but didn't say anything, then she walked to the couch and picked up a leash, which she attached to the front of the collar. She placed a blindfold over my eyes.

"Now slave, we're going downstairs to have some fun. Well, I'm going to have some fun; you're going to learn a lot. Stay on your knees and crawl after me. Come."

She tugged on the leash. I crawled. My ankle cuffs made crawling difficult. When we reached the top of the stairs, she let me sit and guided me down the steps.

Downstairs, she pushed me over some kind of bench. My feet were still on the ground, but my stomach, chest and head were flat against the padded top. Bryn pulled a number of cords around my upper and lower back and tightened them. She undid the cuffs and re-locked my ankles and wrists to the sides of whatever I was resting on. She then ran her fingers over my ass and fondled my balls and cock. I breathed in quickly as my penis stiffened.

She walked around to the front of the bench and removed my blindfold.

"Welcome to my play space!"

Jesus fucking Christ!! What had I gotten myself into?! Who was she?! The room was some type of torture den. The walls were painted a deep purple and there were lit candles everywhere. All around were medieval looking punishment devices. To my left was a large X made out of wood planks, with eye-bolts screwed into the top and bottom. In front of me was a red, plush Victorian chair that looked like a throne. To my right was a long padded table with bolts in the side, no doubt for tying someone down. Against the far wall hung about two dozen different punishment devices. There were paddles and whips of different sizes and thicknesses. There were a number of crops and canes, and several belts. As a finishing touch, directly in front of me on the wall was the classic poster of a kitten hanging from a tree branch, "Hang in there!"

She ran her hand over my butt and up my back to my neck. She knelt down and gently ran her finger down my cheek to my chin.

"Do you like it?" She asked.
I stared at her without answering.

SLAP!

She smacked my face hard.

"Are you stupid?"
I was, actually, very stupid, because I had let a twenty-four year old blackmail me and tie me up in her secret dungeon. But she probably wanted a different answer. I stayed silent.

"That's ok, Taylor. Go ahead. Resist. If it makes you feel better."

She walked to the wall and pulled down a brown leather belt, then knelt by my ear. She cupped my chin and raised my eyes to meet hers.

"Tonight's lessons are discipline and punishment. These will be key elements in your new life." Her breath was hot on my ear. Despite my anger and rising despair, I was hard as a rock.

"First, I'm going to show you discipline." She stood up and walked behind me, letting the belt drag along my back.

"Being a slave will be difficult for you at first; I know that. You're going to make a lot of mistakes." She let the belt trail down between my ass cheeks and over my balls.

"Discipline is how you will learn to serve me better. I will record any infraction you make, and when you reach a certain count, you'll be disciplined, which can take many forms. Think of it as motivation." She began rubbing my ass with the belt.

"Eventually, you'll come to crave it, as you will accept and crave your service to me." She began spanking me with the belt. It wasn't hard, but it wasn't exactly soft, either.

Smack! Smack! Smack! Smack! Smack! Smack! Smack!

The spanking grew in intensity as it went on. I was surprised how much it hurt. I have a pretty high tolerance for pain, or so I thought, but I guess my ass was an exception.

"I see you jumping around and you're probably wondering why this hurts, since I'm not spanking you hard." She put the belt on my lower back and ran her nails over my ass. "You have a lot of nerve endings in your butt. And while I'm warming you up slowly, it's still a shock."

She walked back to the wall and replaced the belt. She grabbed a wooden paddle.

She patted me on the shoulder as she walked by. "This paddle's going to hurt."

Whap!! Whap!! WHAP!!

"Unngh!!!" I hadn't wanted to make a sound and give her the satisfaction. But it hurt like a son of a bitch. Bryn stopped and ran her fingers through my hair.
"Shhhh . . . it's ok. I know it hurts."

Whap!! Whap!! WHAP!!

Whap!! Whap!! WHAP!!

Whap!! Whap!! WHAP!!

"UMmph!" I thrashed and pulled on the chains, but they held.
"Shhh . . . breathe." She said softly. She trailed her fingertips down to my ball sack, then slowly, achingly, over my cock. She walked back to the wall and traded the paddle for a cat-o-nine-tails. Over the next however long, I experienced a tawse, a leather paddle, a standard crop and what she called a lollipop crop, which was a crop with round chip on the end. I don't know how many times she hit me, but my guess was around 100. My ass hurt and I was covered in sweat. I said a small prayer of relief when she returned her implement to the wall and didn't grab another one.

"That is discipline, my love. It will be administered at least twice a week. At the beginning maybe every day. The better you follow my commands, the less discipline I'll have to administer."

She walked back to the wall and took down a thin cane. Oh God! She wasn't done.

"Now punishment is something different." Her tone changed. Before she had spoken like a strict but ultimately caring teacher. Now she just sounded strict. "Punishment is when you are willfully disobedient or commit a serious offense. It is meant to instruct, but through pain." My heart started to pound.

"With discipline there was a warm-up. There were breaks and gentle strokes. Punishment . . ." she let the word hang as she walked behind me.

WHACK!!! WHACK!!! WHACK!!! WHACK!!!
WHACK!!! WHACK!!! WHACK!!! WHACK!!!
WHACK!!! WHACK!!! WHACK!!! WHACK!!!

I didn't scream because it hurt too fucking much to scream. Instead I made strained grunting noises as I struggled vainly against my bonds. My breath was ragged and shallow and I thought for a moment like I was going to pass out. She placed the cane on my lower back and walked around to hold my head with both hands. She looked into my eyes. She looked flushed and she was breathing deeply. At first, I thought she was out of shape, and then it dawned on me: she liked this. She was getting off on it.

"That is punishment. It's not fun. It's not gentle. And that was a very minor punishment. It only gets worse, especially with no warm up." She caressed my face again with her hands, running them over my cheeks, then planted a slow kiss on my forehead. My breath slowly returned to normal.

She returned the cane to the wall, and to my horror came back with the crop.
"So tell me slave. What is discipline?"
"Discipline is to help me do, I mean follow orders better, to be a better slave." I spit out the words in a hurry.

"Is that what I said? Discipline is to help you do, I mean follow orders better, to be a better slave? Is that what I sound like?" She walked around behind me.

Smack! Smack! Smack!

“Aaarrhh!!!”

“How do you address me?"
"Master! Master! I'm sorry, Master. I'm sorry. Discipline is to help me be a better slave, Master. It's to teach me to better follow orders."

"Not exactly, slave" she walked behind me. I tensed up. "But close enough" she lightly patted my ass with the crop. "And what is punishment?"
"Punishment is to ensure I don't make the same mistake twice, Master."
"Good answer, slave. But then again, you *are* smart, right Doctor Clark?"
"Yes, Master."

She transferred me to the padded table, first handcuffing my hands behind my back and my ankles together before untying the ropes and helping me shuffle to the next location of torture. I winced as she pushed me back onto my beaten ass. She bound me to the table face up with more ropes. Whoever had taught her knots had done a good job.

She ran her hands over my body, down my chest and legs, down to my feet. She tested if I was ticklish and where. She moved slowly up my thighs and watched my reactions as she came close to my cock. She played with my nipples, experimenting just how hard she had to squeeze until I arched my body to try to escape the pain. Her hands never broke contact with my body for ten excruciating, wonderful minutes.

"What type of owner would I be," she began, "if I didn't know my slave's body. What he likes" she ran her hand softly over my nipple, "what causes him pain," she grabbed my balls and squeezed until I yelled. "And what makes him excited and willing to do anything I want," she ran her hands around my thighs in slow circles. She leaned over the table, bringing her mouth achingly close to my erection. She spoke in sultry whisper.

"Do you want me, slave?" Slowly she brought her lips to the underside of my cock, right below the head, and gave it a brief kiss. Her hair fell down and touched my shaft. I closed my eyes.

"No, slave, look at me. I know how badly you want me. You've tried to fight it. But I saw it when we first met. I saw it every time we talked." As she spoke, I felt her breath on me.

"Do you want me to me stroke you, slave? Is that what you want?"
I warred against myself. I hated her, but without question, this was the most erotic experience I'd ever had.

"What would you do for me? Anything? Would you be my slave?" She moved her head away from my crotch and climbed up onto my stomach. She pressed her groin down onto me. She was wet right through her panties. She put her hands on my cheeks and stared into my eyes.

"This is what you want. Deep down you know it. Even if you're just realizing it now, as your cock begs and strains for my attention, as you fight with your own ego about submitting fully to me. You know in that place you rarely go, that you want to be my slave."

I had been betrayed, blackmailed, beaten and slapped that evening, but hearing this speech was the closest I came to crying. But I held on.

"I see you fighting it. Let go, Taylor. Give in to what you want. You will love being my slave so much more than you ever enjoyed being free."

I looked deep into her eyes.
“Fuck. You.”

I twisted to try to break her gaze. She gripped the sides of my face harder. Her face lost its loving expression as she clenched her teeth. She spoke sternly.

"I'll tell you what, Taylor. I'm going to reach my hand back to your groin, and if your dick's not hard, I'll let you go. I'll give you all the recordings and you can return to your normal life of fucking dumb girls and feeling lonely. All you have to do is lose the erection."

I don't think she would've let me go anyway, but it didn't matter. I was rock hard. She smiled, then leaned forward and kissed me slowly. I wanted to hate her then, to rail against her, but I couldn't.

"You've been a good slave for your first night, and I know how difficult this is for you. Maybe I'll let you come." She slid off the table and walked down next to my groin. She licked the tip of her index finger and slowly rubbed it in a circle underneath the head of my penis.

"Does this feel good, slave?"
"Yes, Master."
"Do you want me to continue?"
"Yes, Master."
"You are not to cum without my permission, ever. I will let you know if you can cum tonight. Nod yes."

I nodded. I would have nodded to anything. She kept rubbing in a circle. I felt the beginning of my orgasm in my balls. Precum was forming on the head of my cock. Oh my God it felt so good! If she kept this up for just a little while longer I would explode.

She sensed it, too, and let go of me. She walked to a cupboard and pulled out a bottle of lube and put on a thin rubber glove. She poured some into her hands and rubbed it in as she came back to the table and kissed my stomach. She began stroking me again. She read my body's reactions, varying the strength of her grip to keep me on the edge of orgasm.

She pressed my penis up against my stomach as she licked and sucked on my balls. Then she squirted more lube on her fingers and ran them up and down my ass crack. Her gloved finger found my asshole, and she made tiny circles as she applied a steady pressure.

"Have you ever had anything up here, slave?"
"No, Master."

She kept circling with her finger, pressing harder and harder. I wouldn't have stopped her if I could. Her finger went inside of me.

"Oh! Master!"
I felt her smile. "I'm going to forgive that little outburst, slave."
"Thank you, Master."
"This is your prostate, slave. I can tell you love it: your dick is leaking precum right now."

I arched my back.

"What a little slut you are, slave! I had no idea." With her other hand she reached over and gave me three quick, firm pumps, bringing me right to the edge of orgasm. Then she let go and pulled her other finger out of my ass. She walked over to the counter and threw away the glove. I could barely see straight.

"Please, Master!"
"Oh, slave. She leaned down and brought her lips close to my ear. "I own you. That means I own your cock and all your orgasms. I decide if and when you cum. And right now I think you owe me an apology for speaking out of turn."
"I'm sorry, Master. I'm sorry for speaking out of turn. But-"
"Shhh . . . she pushed her finger over my lips."

She straightened up and walked out of the room. All of my senses were heightened. I could feel the air against my skin and hear the faint buzzing of the light overhead. My mind raced, but I couldn't focus on any one thing.

Again, I don't know how much time passed. Maybe five minutes, maybe twenty. My internal sense of time was all askew. Everything was askew. My dick had finally softened, though it still felt sensitive. My balls hurt.

I head the click clack of Bryn's heels. My dick stiffened before she even entered the room.

She walked in carrying a bag of ice, which she placed on my cock and balls.

"Stop screaming! It's ice. You've felt ice before."

Bryn stood next to the table looking down at me as I panted and tried to catch my breath. She lifted up the bag and peaked underneath, then let it fall back on top of me.

"Ok, I admit. It's probably cold." She smiled, then walked over to the cupboard and grabbed a few things. When she returned, she held up a plastic tube and ring contraption.

"Do you know what this is?"
"No, Master."
"It's a chastity device. It will keep you from playing with my cock when I'm not watching you. You have a masturbation problem, obviously, or you wouldn't be in this mess. This will serve as my guarantee that you'll be ready and willing any time I need you. It will also help you realize and accept that you're my property and that you exist first and foremost to serve me. Nod yes."

I nodded. She removed the bag of ice. My dick had done its impression of a scared turtle, shriveling up to about half its normal flaccid size.

"Here we go." She said. The ring opened, and she fit it around my ball sack. It was like a firm grip on the base of my nuts. Then she fit the plastic tube over my dick and pressed it against the ring. She fit a small cylindrical piece of plastic through a hole in both the ring and tube, joining them together. To finish, she pushed a small lock through a hole in the end of the cylinder, trapping everything in place.

"Here's my favorite sound," she said, and closed the lock with an audible click. She looked at her handy work, then patted the top of my device.

"Don't ever ask me to take off your chastity device. I'll decide when you cum. And if you pester me about it, I'll make sure you wait another week. Understood?"
"Yes, Master."

"Good. Now, as well as me knowing about my slave, my slave should know all about me. Tonight, you're going to learn my scent." She pulled out a roll of tape and taped my mouth shut. She then retrieved the blindfold I had worn earlier and put it over my eyes.

"You've earned the privilege of smelling me, slave, but not seeing or tasting me. Those will come in time, probably." I heard her taking off some of her clothing, then felt her climb onto the table and straddle my head. She lowered her pussy right above my nose.

"Inhale me, slave. Smell your Goddess and owner."

Even before she climbed onto the table I could smell her arousal. Now it was overpowering. She smelled deep and dark, and beautiful.

"That's right, slave." She rocked back and forward on my face, then put her palms on my chest and pinched my nipples. Her breathing increased as she ground her hips into me.

"Mmmm! "Oh yes! Oh, fuck!" She ground harder and raked her nails across my stomach and chest.

"Smell me you fucking slut! You whore! You want me so fucking bad you can't stop masturbating with my towel, you fucking bitch! You thought you were hiding it from me you stupid fucking slut! Oh! God! I’m going to do horrible things to you. I’m going to humiliate you.” Her knees pressed against the sides of my head. "You're my fucking slave now! You're . . . oh . . . my . . . slave. My . . . oh! OH! OH!" Her body shivered and convulsed as she moaned. She ground her hips into me, hard, and then yelled out. Her body spasmed then stopped. She leaned forward, resting her head against my stomach. When she spoke again, she was still breathing heavily.

"Mmmm . . . that was nice slave. It's so nice to release all that pent up sexual energy. Phew!" She climbed off me, then bent down and patted my cheek.

"I'm going to get a drink of water, and I might take a little nap." I heard her walk to the door. "Don't go anywhere."

Chapter 5

I lay on the table, trying and failing to not think about what just happened: the beating, the chastity device now encasing my dick, the way my body had responded to Bryn. I imagined saying no when Bryn asked to shower at my place. Then I wouldn’t be tied blindfolded and naked to a table in her dungeon, smelling the scent of her pussy and feeling welts rising on my butt. It didn't make anything better.

I didn't know if this was just going to be a kinky weekend or if she really thought she could make me her slave. She couldn't possibly, right? She wasn't a sociopath: she was deep down a nice girl who just has some interesting kinks. I tried to believe it fully, but some part of me had seen her eyes and heard her voice when she spoke.

I heard her coming down the stairs. My cock tried to harden, but the chastity device wouldn't let it. It hurt. She walked to the table and ripped the tape off my mouth. My anger came back to me, and I tried and failed to keep it out of my voice.

"Miss me?"
"Yes, Master."
Bryn grew serious. She looked down at my encased cock.
"Does it hurt, slave?"
"Yes, Master."
"You know what would really hurt?"
"No, Master."
"If I got the lollipop crop and beat your balls till they were black and blue."
I didn't feel like that was a question, so I kept quiet.

"Would you like that?"
"No, Master."
"Good, because I have plans for those balls that would be ruined if I mashed them to a pulp." She leaned forward and gave my balls a quick kiss, sending more pain up my stomach. "We're going to take some pictures now. You won't like them, but you're going to be an enthusiastic participant because you don't want your balls mashed. Nod yes."
I nodded.
"Good." She climbed onto the table and sat on my chest, then removed my blindfold. She was holding a camera, and around her waist she wore a harness with a life-like dildo, complete with veins.
"Do you like my cock, slave? Be honest."
I stared at her without speaking. I imagined getting my hands around her throat. She climbed off of me and grabbed a small leather paddle from the wall.

Whap!

She hit my balls. I screamed.

Whap!

She hit them again. My anger turned to pain, and fear. She was fucking insane!

“Let’s try again. Do you like my cock?”
"No, Master."
"Is it because my cock is bigger than your average size cock?"
My cock was slightly above average, though you couldn't tell now that it was trapped in plastic.
"No, Master. I just don't like cocks."

"That's a very bad attitude, slave. Fortunately for you, I'm going to help you get past it."
She climbed back on top of me.
"Kiss the tip." She pushed it against my lips. I hesitated for an instant, and her face tightened. I knew that look. I quickly kissed the tip. There was something sticky on it.
"Good boy. Kiss it again and keep kissing it." As I did, she took some pictures. "Now open your mouth." She slid the dildo into my mouth. It was honey. She had coated the dildo with honey. "Now suck it. Suck the honey off my cock." More pictures were taken.
"Ohhh, that feels good. Can you deep throat my cock, slave? Can you take all eight inches?"
I started gagging when she got about halfway in, so the answer was no, I couldn't. Bryn slowly pushed in about three inches and then held it in place. After a moment she slowly rocked forward, stopping just before I gagged, then pulled it almost all the way out. Then slowly back in until I almost gagged, then back out.
When she'd decided she'd gotten enough pictures, she slid off me.
"What do you say?"
"Thank you, Master."
"For what?"
"Thank you, Master, for letting me suck your cock."
"Your welcome, slave."

She left the room. When she came back, she chained my ankles together and unfastened the ropes binding me to the table. She took the rope of one wrist and attached it to my ankle. She did the same with the other wrist and had me sit up. She handcuffed my hands together in front of me and undid the locks connecting my wrists and ankles. She attached the leash to my collar.

"Get down on all fours. Crawl after me."

She took me upstairs to a guest room on the second floor. Her bedroom was down the hall, but I was told I hadn't earned permission to enter it. In the guest room was a four-poster bed, a leather reading chair and, unfortunately, a 4 by 4 foot cage.

I thought I might be going in the cage, but she pushed me onto the bed and climbed on top of me. She began kissing me passionately and grinding against my imprisoned cock. She kissed me all over my face and neck. She thrust her tongue into my mouth. She pulled my hair and pressed her forehead against mine.

"Oh, my sweet slave. Oh darling! You're doing so well tonight! I know it's hard. Kiss me, slave. Kiss me."

I kissed her. I'd like to say I didn't enjoy it, but that would be a lie.

"Come, I'm going to sit on the chair in the corner and we're going to talk. You can ask me any questions you want, and I won't beat you unless you're disrespectful." She led me to the corner, where she sat in the black leather chair and I knelt at her feet. "Kiss my feet to start, slave. This is your way of thanking me for this privilege. Then you may begin. You can also address me as Bryn for this short period."

I kissed her feet, then sat back on my heels.

"Why, Bryn?"
"I already answered that. Are you going to waste this opportunity asking me things you already know? Because we don't have to do this."

"No, I'm sorry. I guess, I meant, isn't this extreme? You're beating me and you've locked up my cock. Is this really – I mean – is this how it's going to be?"
"Taylor. I know it's difficult now, but that's just because you haven't earned any privileges. You can't talk without permission because you haven't showed me that you can handle it. In time, if you're obedient, you will get to talk without being spoken to. For now, though, yes, this is how it's going to be."
"Will I have any freedom? Am I going to be in handcuffs and naked always?"
"You will have freedoms as I see fit. You will be in handcuffs when I want you to be, and yes, you'll almost always be naked when you're here."
"Are you going to put me in that cage?"
"I am."
"Is there any way I can convince you of the feelings I have for you? You know I'm in love with you, Bryn; you knew it when we first met. You don't have to do this. I was always yours for the taking. Let me show you how happy I can make you. I can love you, Bryn, truly."

She looked down. I saw her face flush as her lips slightly parted. She looked at me and smiled.
"You are one smooth talker, lover. How many women have you gotten into bed with that silver tongue."
"I don't know . . . 20?"
"Would you like me to get my cane and beat the truth out of you?"
“I don't know how many. Over 50. I stopped counting. I didn't have a steady girlfriend. I'm not some player. Bryn, you're a good read of people, I know you are. Look at me. You know I'm in love with you, Bryn. I can tell.”

Her face softened, just a little. Then she reached forward to pat my cheek.
"Nice try, slave. But no, I don't buy it."

"You fucking bitch! This is illegal! Let me go you fucking cunt!!"

She stood up and slapped my face with her right hand, first forehand, then backhand. She had put her weight behind it and it hurt.

"What are you going to do about it, Taylor?! Take me to court? The brilliant Dr. Taylor Clark was made an involuntary slave by his 24 year-old student. Here are the pictures and films she used to blackmail him. What news outlet wouldn't eat this story up? It would go viral in a minute. You won't go to the cops because I would just show them those threatening emails and say I had no choice. Besides, who's going to believe you? It'll be your word against mine, and I think you know how convincing I can be."

She slapped me twice again. This time I fell over.

"You stupid bitch! You thought I was really crying in your car when I told you you were mean to me. How dumb are you?! Jen told me you practically cried when I didn't show up to the next class. You kept staring at the door like some pathetic teenager, hoping I'd show up. You're not going to talk your way out of this, Taylor. You're mine now, and you better get used to it. You think I've been a bitch tonight?! Call me a cunt again and you'll see just how big a bitch I can be!"

She was breathing heavily and her eyes were piercing and angry. I stared at the floor. When she had calmed down a little, she spoke coldly.

"Anything else before the silence vow goes back into place?"
"I thought you said you rented the ground floor from an elderly couple."
"I lied."
"Why?"
"It fit the story better. I didn't want you to know I have a lot of money. I felt like it. Take your pick. Question and answer time is over. Get up. You're going to the bathroom and then getting in the cage."

She watched as I peed, which she made me do sitting down. I brushed my teeth. She then led me back to the guest room and opened the door to the cage. There were two blankets in there.

"Get in. You're spending the night in here for the time being."

I crawled in and curled up as best I could. She shut the cage door and locked it from the outside. I looked up at her as she stood over the cage.

"You've pissed me off. Tomorrow you're going to pay for it."

I wasn't going to answer. She could beat me senseless if she wanted, but screw her, I wasn't going to apologize. I just wanted to curl up and go to sleep. Maybe she sensed it. Maybe she was just tired. She let it go, though, at least for the time being. She turned off the light and shut the door.

The cage was cramped, and I was irritated and despondent and every other emotion I could think of. My ass hurt, my cock hurt, and my face hurt. But mostly my pride hurt. I tried not to think about Bryn, and how easily I'd believed all her lies. What would she do to me? Did she really mean what she was saying? My mind ran in circles for what seemed like an hour, until, mercifully, I feel asleep.

Chapter 6

The pain in my cock woke me the next morning. I had no doubt been having an erotic dream where I didn't let myself get blackmailed by my sociopathic student. I moved around as best I could in the cage, which wasn't much. With a little trouble, I could switch from curled on my left side to curled on my right. My legs were cramped and every part of me hurt. And I had to go the bathroom.

Yelling for Bryn wouldn't get me anything but a beating, so I kept quiet. She would let me out exactly when she wanted to and not a moment sooner. I had resigned myself to letting Bryn think she'd broken me. I didn't really have a choice. If she wanted me to call her Master and hear how much I loved being her slave, so be it. I'd figure a way out eventually. And when I did, she was going to suffer.

I heard her come out of her bedroom and go into the bathroom. I could hear the faucet running. I went from having to piss to *really* having to piss. I let my hopes rise when the bathroom door opened, but Bryn walked downstairs. I think she made herself breakfast. By the time she finally came upstairs I was rocking back and forth, clamping my piss muscle as tight as I could. She walked in and circled the cage without speaking. She was wearing a black silk robe with a colorful Asian design on the back. She stopped and looked down at me.

"Did you pee on yourself?"
"No Master."
"Do you have to pee now?"
"Yes Master."

"Pee sitting down, then take a cold shower. Shave, brush your teeth and meet me downstairs. There's a towel on the bathroom counter. You have ten minutes. Before you go I need to take your collar off."

Bryn unlocked the cage and I twisted my way out. She unlatched my collar and I crawled on cramped legs to the bathroom. A hot shower would have been wonderful, but no doubt she would check on me. I take quick showers when they're cold, and I made it downstairs with a minute to spare.

Bryn was standing in the living room with her arms crossed over her chest. She was still wearing her robe, but had put on high heels. She held a crop in her right hand. She didn't look pleased. I stood before her with my hands over my groin.

"Whap!"

The crop bit into my thigh. I jumped and turned.

"Don't move! Don't ever try to avoid discipline."
I turned back to face her.

"Whap! Whap! Whap!" The blows came down on my thighs, one after the other.

"Take your hands away from my cock. Don't ever cover yourself unless I tell you too."

I moved my hands away.

Whap!

"When you enter a room, you get down on your hands and knees and give each of my feet one kiss. Then you wait for instruction. Go upstairs, then come down and try it again."

I ran upstairs, then turned around and came downstairs, knelt before her and kissed each of her feet. I waited for instructions. After thirty seconds I looked up at her.

"Whap!"

"Keep your head down. I'll give you instructions when I'm ready."

She reattached my collar and walked around me.

"This position you're in is called present" she pronounced it pre-SENT. "When I say "present," you get down on your hands and knees with your head down. Stand up."

I stood.

"Present."

I got down on my hands and knees.

"WHAP!"

"Not fast enough. Try again. Up." I stood. "Present."

I got down on my hands and knees.

Whap!

"Stop thinking. When I give you an order, you do it. You don't stop to think about it. Try again. Up . . . Present."

I dove to my hands and knees.

"Better. Try again. Up."

We tried it again, and again, and again.

"Your next position is "down." When I say down, you get on your hands and knees and press your forehead to the floor . . . down!"

I dove to the floor and pressed my forehead against her rug.

Whap!

"Up. Try again . . . down!"

I did it again.

Whap!

"You're thinking again. Up. Do it again."

Over and over it went. I next learned "kneel," which was me sitting on my heels, then "foot," which was me on my hands and knees, holding my lips to her left foot. She drilled me until my knees were red and aching from throwing myself on the floor as quickly as possible. When she was satisfied, she sat on the couch and motioned me to kneel before her.

"You're learning. I know this isn't easy or fun for you, but it's necessary. I won't have a lazy slave. What do you say?"
"Thank you, Master."
"Slave look at me."

I did. She took my chin in her hand.

"You know you have punishment coming for last night. Crawl downstairs. Go in the dungeon and place yourself over the spanking horse."

I hesitated. I didn't want punishment. I didn't want the cane again.

"Slave, you've got three seconds to get moving or your punishment doubles."

I quickly crawled downstairs and put myself over the bench and waited. Bryn took her time coming down. When she finally arrived, she placed her computer on a chair in front of me, then she cinched me to the bench with rope and cuffed my hands and feet. She grabbed a cane from the wall and placed it on my back. I flinched with the memory of what that cane could do. I could still feel the striped welts from last night.

"I want to show you some of your pictures from our photo session," she said. "I think you may have a career in modeling ahead of you." She touched my nose with the tip of her index finger and slid her chair right in front of me. She opened the computer, and soon there was a picture on the screen of me sucking what looked like a real cock.

"Look at those big blow job lips of yours!" She laughed at her own joke, then clicked through the photo book she had made of me fellating her dildo. She knew what she was doing: almost every picture hid the harness she was wearing and any sign of her feminine hands. It just looked like me sucking cock.

"I'm going to get these ready to email, too, just in case you decide slavery's not for you."

I thrashed against the cuffs and the ropes. I wanted to get at her. I didn't care what happened. I just wanted to get my hands around her throat.

"Calm down, slave. These don't have to go out to anyone. But you need to understand who's in control and why." She closed the computer and put it under her chair. Then she knelt and held my face in her hands.

"I won't show anyone these pictures, Taylor. I promise. Not unless you run off or try something stupid."
I kept thrashing. I was beyond where words could reach me.

SLAP!

"Enough. I get it. You're mad. But this is your life now, Taylor. You're my slave, and you do as I say. Unless you want me to use that cane on your balls instead of your ass, you better calm down."

I would get her. Somehow.

The cane had fallen on the floor. She picked it up and walked behind me.

SMACK!! SMACK!! SMACK!! SMACK!! SMACK!!
SMACK!! SMACK!! SMACK!! SMACK!! SMACK!!
SMACK!! SMACK!! SMACK!! SMACK!! SMACK!!
SMACK!! SMACK!! SMACK!! SMACK!! SMACK!!

I forgot my anger and everything else. I couldn't think. I couldn't see. I couldn't speak. All I could do was try to breathe and take the pain. I tried to send my mind elsewhere, but it was too much. I found my voice and screamed and screamed.

I lay there, panting as Bryn fetched something from the cupboard. She then unlocked my chastity tube and slid it off me. Oh my God! The relief! She rubbed lotion onto my cock and balls. Her touch was heavenly. She massaged every inch of me, spending a lot of time on the head of my cock. I felt the first stirrings of an orgasm when she pulled away.

"Thank you Master."
"You're welcome, slave."

She sat in the chair facing me.

"No matter what happens, slave, you're not to break eye contact with me."

It was then I started to feel the heat in my crotch. It started slowly, warmly, but quickly heated up. The lotion she had rubbed all over me was some type of athletic gel like Ben Gay or Icy Hot. My eyes widened and I started squirming. My entire groin felt like it was on fire!

I stared at Bryn, or tried to through watery eyes. I wasn't crying, but the pain was making my eyes tear. Bryn was staring at me without smiling, breathing deeply. She opened up her robe, revealing black lace panties and a matching bra. She slowly rubbed her left nipple, never breaking eye contact with me. He lips parted slightly.

I groaned as a wave of pain passed through my testicles. It felt like I'd gotten kicked in the balls. I gritted my teeth and struggled to keep my eyes on hers.

She slowly moved her hand down her stomach to her panties and began rubbing in slow circles. It felt like a thousand needles were stabbing me! I moaned softly, then louder. Bryn rocked forward and back in the chair. The look on her face was positively feral. I tried to hold it but I couldn't. I screamed. Bryn gasped and put her hand inside her panties.

She got off on this: seeing me in pain, hurting me! I would never be able to talk my way out of punishment from Bryn. I wouldn't be able to soothe her anger because it wasn't anger that motivated her to punish me. It was lust. I cried out as another wave of pain seared through my groin. Bryn moved her fingers in and out of herself. I screamed and screamed, and soon she joined me, cumming thunderously as I thrashed in my bonds.

She sat for a while in the chair, staring at me, catching her breath. Then walked to me and placed her fingers against my nose.

"Smell me."

I did. I would do anything to keep from experiencing that pain again. I worried that it had burned the nerve endings in my dick and left me impotent. She had pictures of me sucking a dildo. Fine. It was enraging, but she already had blackmail material on me. I just had to find a way out.

She reattached my chastity tube before untying me from the bench. I sank to my knees and kissed her feet.

"Thank you for punishing me Master."
"You're welcome slave." She grabbed a crop from the wall, attached the leash to my collar and headed for the door. I crawled after her. "Follow me. It's time to get you something to eat."

I crawled behind Bryn as she walked slowly to the kitchen. She was carrying her robe, which left me a clear view of her beautiful ass in her lace panties. How could I think of her as anything more than an evil bitch? How could I be attracted to her? But I was. I pictured making love to her. I imagined her body beneath mine and ramming my cock into her while she moaned.

"Down."

I pressed my head against the floor automatically. Bryn must have been satisfied, because she didn't beat me or make me do it again, and I smiled a little. Then I realized what I was smiling about and felt disgusting. Bryn came around and handcuffed my wrists behind my back.

I stayed with my head down while Bryn scraped something into what I guessed was a bowl. It had been close to twenty-four hours since I last ate anything. I was starving.

"Kneel."

I rose to my knees. Bryn placed a bowl of oatmeal on the floor in front of me. She stood watching me, taking delight in my horror as I realized she wanted me to eat from the bowl on the floor like a dog. That fucking bitch. She wouldn't stop until she had humiliated me in every way possible. But I wouldn't let it affect me. I would do what she wanted without giving her the satisfaction of hearing me whine and moan. I put my face in the bowl and took a bite.

"WHAP!! WHAP!!"

The crop bit into my already sore ass. I screamed!

"Ooooowwww!! Why Master?! What did I do wrong?!"
"You don't eat until I say eat. It doesn't matter that the food is in front of you. You stay in position until I let you move."
"I'm sorry Master. I didn't know."
"No, you didn't know, but any halfwit could have figured it out. Am I going to have to tell you how to do everything?"
"No, Master."
"Then act like it. Show some intuition, use your brain. Eventually I would like to not have to give you orders all day long."
"I'm sorry, Master."

I sat back on my heels and waited. I looked up at her. "Head down!" She snapped.

She waited for what seemed like a good minute.

"Eat." I sank into the cold oatmeal and ate it. It wasn't good, but it was food. It was just hard to keep my face from falling into the bowl with my hands cuffed behind my back. As I ate, I heard her run the faucet, and she placed a bowl of water next to the oatmeal. When I had finished the oatmeal she patted my head.

"Good boy. Now drink."
I put my face into the bowl of water and lapped it up. I hadn't realized how thirsty I was until I started drinking. I drank it as fast as I could, which was still slowly.

"Down."
I stopped drinking and put my forehead on the floor. "Slave, I'm going for a jog. While I'm gone, clean the bathroom off the living room and the guest bathroom upstairs. I want them spotless. There are supplies under the sink."

She uncuffed my wrists and recuffed them in front of me. Then she headed upstairs to change as I found the right cleaning supplies and headed towards the bathroom. As I was beginning, she came downstairs in shorts, running shoes, and a t-shirt. She stood in front of me, then looked down at her feet. I sank to my knees and kissed her shoes.

"Good boy."
"Thank you, Master."

While Bryn jogged, I cleaned the bathrooms. I knew she wanted me to do a bad job, so she could make me do it again and beat me, but I wouldn't let her find fault with my work. I scrubbed the shower tiles and cleaned out the medicine cabinets, wiping down the shelves. I made sure the handles in the sink and shower were shining.

Bryn came back just as I was finishing downstairs. She made me wait in the down position while she inspected my work.

"Slave, I'm impressed. I thought you'd suck at cleaning. But this is good work. I'm going to give you a little reward." She had me follow her into the guest bedroom, where I'd spent the night trapped in her cage. She sat down on the bed and had me take off her shoes.

"I'm going to let you clean me after my jog. Isn't that exciting, slave?"
"Yes, Master."
"Start at my feet and slowly lick the sweat off me."

Her voice was so arrogant. My dick, against all common sense, tried to harden in its tube. At least it still worked.

I bent down and gently kissed each foot. Then I took her left foot in my hands and slowly licked up the sole. I took her smallest toe into my mouth and sucked it gently.

"Ooohh, slave, that's good. Make sure you lick between each toe."

Her feet stunk, but I sucked each toe into my mouth and swirled my tongue around it, then pushed my tongue between her toes and licked up the sweat and dirt that had settled there. All the while, Bryn hummed contentedly. I licked her soles and her heels.

"Good job, slave. Now come up here and lick my armpits clean. I think they're pretty ripe."

She removed her t-shirt, leaving her in just a sports bra. I stared at her breasts.

She snapped her fingers, bring me back to the present. “I know they're nice, but you have work to do."

She lifted her right arm above her head and lay back on the bed. I dove into her armpit. She giggled as I lapped up her sweat. She was a little stinky, but it was an almost pleasant odor.

"Now the left, slave."

I moved to her left. She ran her fingers through my hair with her right hand.

"Now lie down on the bed on your back. I want to give you another reward for doing such a good job and not being as much of a whiny little bitch as before.”

My cock started to twitch. I quickly lay on the bed and let her cuff my wrists and ankles to the posts on each corner. She ran downstairs and came back with the key to my chastity belt and unlocked me. My dick sprang into an erection immediately. She slowly rubbed it with her fingers.

"Your cock is so responsive!" She ran one finger up and down my shaft. I moaned against my will.

"I'm going to let you taste me now, slave. Is that something you want?"
"Yes, Master." My cocked jumped at the idea of eating her pussy. I didn't care that she was sweaty.
"Good, slave." She stopped rubbing me and stood by the bed.

"Look at me, slave." She hooked her thumbs into her shorts and underwear and pushed them off her onto the ground. Her pubic hair was neatly trimmed. Then she removed her top. Her breasts barely moved. She stood before me naked. She was the most beautiful woman I had ever seen, and for a moment being her slave seemed like a fair trade to spend any time at all with her.

She climbed onto the bed and turned so that she stood facing my feet. She then placed her hands on my chest and lowered herself on top of me.

"I'm very sweaty back there, slave, so make sure you lick up all the sweat before you stick your tongue inside me."

I waited for her to bring her pussy to my face, but the angle was wrong. She sat back and brought her ass to my mouth.

"Taste me slave. Lick your owner's ass."

She was so cruel, so crushingly cruel. She lifted her ass up just a bit and spoke to me.

"Slave. You're either going to lick my asshole now, or after I beat you bloody. I know you want to preserve your dignity by pretending to put up a fight, but understand this: you don't have any dignity. You're my slave. So get that tongue out and start licking my asshole before I lose my temper."

She lowered her ass back to my face and I stuck out my tongue and licked. I went from bottom to top, pushing my tongue into her crack and licking up the sweat. She sighed. Her ass smelled faintly of shit. I licked bottom to top again, then rested the tip of my tongue against her asshole. I flicked it twice.

"Slave! That feels good. Do it again."

I did it again and she giggled. I licked up and down her crack again.

"All this foreplay is nice, slave, but get that tongue inside me."

I brought my tongue back to her sphincter and pressed. She squirmed a bit and then moaned loudly as my tongue popped inside her.

"Lick, slave. I said you were going to taste me. Now taste me."

As I licked, she leaned forward and stroked my dick with her hand. Then she pressed her lips to my stomach and gave me a hickey right above my waist.

Her hand on my cock had me pushing my tongue into her as far as it could go. She moved her ass in a small circle. If I could get her to lose control of herself, maybe she'd let me orgasm.

She grabbed my balls in her fist. "Don't stop!"

I didn't stop as she sat up. Her body started to rock faster and I knew she was playing with her clit.

"Ohhhhhh, yes."

I licked and sucked her asshole as she brought herself to an explosive orgasm. She screamed and pressed down onto me. She dug her nails into my chest.

I kept licking.

"Keep licking my ass you dirty fucking slave." She pushed her ass down harder, and I tried to push my tongue farther up inside her. "God! That feels good you fucking whore!" She exhaled and rested her head on my thigh and blew lightly on my dick. She climbed off me, then bent down and ran her tongue up the underside of my cock. It felt like she had plugged me into a socket. My body spasmed.

"You're a dirty motherfucker, Taylor. You like this." She walked out of the room.

I stared up at the ceiling. Her footsteps went down the hall, stopped, and grew louder as she walked back into the room. She picked up her underwear from the floor and crushed it into a ball.

"Open your mouth."

She stuffed her sweaty underwear into my mouth.

"Those stay in your mouth." She kissed me on the forehead, then gave me a pat on the cheek and left.

Chapter 7

I woke up to the sound of my chastity belt lock clicking shut. Bryn gave my balls a few friendly pats. She pulled her underwear out of my mouth and then untied my hands and feet.

"Crawl to the bathroom and brush your teeth. Then meet me downstairs."

In the living room downstairs, I kissed her feet.

WHAP!

I knew better than ask why.

WHAP!

"Do you want to know why I'm hitting you?"
"Yes Master."

WHAP!

"What was the last thing you did?"
"Kissed your foot."

WHAP!

"Before that."
"Brushed my teeth."

WHAP!

"Keep going"
"Licked your ass."
"There you go! You do remember!"

WHAP!

I kissed her foot.
"Thank you for letting me lick your ass, Master."
"Your welcome slave." She picked up the leash off the table and attached it to my collar, then walked towards the computer room. I crawled after her. She was wearing her robe, which came down to her mid thigh, and I stared at her toned, perfect legs as she walked.

"One of these days, if you're good, I'm going to let you eat my pussy. When that happens, you better know what you're doing. I don't want you groping around wildly or changing your rhythm just when I'm starting to like it. So you're taking an online class in pussy eating, starting now."

She moved the chair out from in front of the computer and had me kneel on a small rug. She hit play on her computer and a clip that looked like homemade porn from the early 90s came on screen. A woman with a short, dirty-blonde mullet was being eaten out by another woman with a short, dirty-blonde mullet. The room was poorly lit and no one was wearing any make-up. Watching it was like taking an anti-erection pill. Dirty-blonde haired mullet woman number 1 started screaming and moaning and oh, oh, oh-ing. Then, in what must have originally been a joke, the screen faded to a woman with short brown hair wearing a vest, standing in front of a chalkboard with a vagina drawn on it.

"Would you like to learn how to bring your partner to incredible heights of erotic ecstasy?"
"Sure," I thought. "Why not?"

The clip was 25 minutes long and was mostly introductory. It showed some tongue-strengthening exercises and, truth be told, had some good advice. I'd gotten good reviews from my tongue-work by other women, but my guess was Bryn would say I wasn't good enough.

When it was over, I crawled out to the living room. Bryn was reading a book. I kissed her feet.

"How was it, slave?"
"Good, Master."
"Tell me three things you learned."
"Turns out women have this thing called a clit. And get this, they like having it licked!”

Bryn laughed. It was an unselfconscious loud, deep-throated laugh. She cupped my chin in her hand and gave me a kiss on the forehead.

"I knew I kept you around for something. Now, seriously, tell me what you learned. Three things."

I told her, and she then made me do the tongue strengthening exercises. When it was done she led me to the kitchen and let me drink water out of my bowl on the floor. Then I fixed her lunch.

"Are you hungry, slave?"
"Yes, Master."
"Why didn't you say so?"

I felt like this was a trap, so I didn't answer.

WHAP!

"Answer me!"
"I didn't think I had a right to ask! I figured you would feed me when you felt I deserved it."

WHAP! WHAP! WHAP!

"That's for not answering me when I asked you a question."
"I'm sorry, Master. I thought it was rhetorical."
"I don't ask rhetorical questions. When I ask you something, you answer."
"Yes, Master."
"I shouldn't feed you for being so disrespectful, but I'm going to show you how nice I am."

She took out some broccoli, hummus, cucumbers and olives and poured them into a blender with some water. She then blended everything into thick, disgusting-looking paste and poured it into a bowl by her feet. I waited. She then pushed her dirty foot into the bowl, getting the paste all over her foot and in between her toes.

"Lick your lunch off my foot, slave."

Of course, she wasn't happy just humiliating me by making me lick my lunch off her foot: she moved her foot around and made me chase it. I must have looked pathetic, lunging after her foot with my mouth. Every once in a while she'd let me catch her foot and I'd quickly take a few licks before she'd move it again. She thought it was really funny, and kept laughing each time I lurched forward and missed her foot. It was just one more little humiliation, and it was far from the most humiliating thing she'd made me do, but after a couple minutes I'd had enough. I sat back on my heels.

"What's the matter, slave?"
"I'm done, Master."
She stopped laughing and her face turned serious.
"Is that right?"
"Yes, Master."

She picked up the bowl and dumped it onto her kitchen floor. She stood and walked toward the sink, holding the bowl upside down. My lunch made a thin line from where I knelt to the counter.
"Lick all of it up. Clean the floor with your tongue. I don't want to see one speck of it left."

She walked out of the room.

I thought about just walking out. What was the worst she could do? But then I knew the worst she could do and it was pretty bad. I started licking. There was no satisfying her. Whatever I did, she'd find fault. My lunch was disgusting when I had to lick it off her foot. It was even more disgusting off the floor.

Bryn walked back into the room with handcuffs and cuffed my hands behind my back, which made licking up my food ten times harder. I had to push my forehead against the floor so I wouldn't fall onto my face. Bryn stood watching me. When I had finished and she inspected my work, she grabbed my hair and lifted me so I was kneeling on my knees. She was pissed off. I was pissed off, too.

"Are you an idiot?"
"No, Master?"

"Do you like being punished? Do you want more beatings?"

SLAP!

She slapped me hard across the face.
"What did I say about answering me!"
"No matter what I say, I'm wrong! You want an excuse to beat me? Go ahead and beat me, but don't pretend you were going to do something else if only I hadn't fucked up."

SLAP! SLAP!

I fell over on my side and curled into a ball. Bryn stood over me.

"You must be an idiot, Taylor. Because I've made it pretty clear what our positions are. You're my slave. You do what I want, when I want it, without sulking or whining like a little bitch."

She grabbed my leash and pulled.
"Upstairs, now."

She led me up to the guest room and put me in the cage with my head towards the back. My hands were still cuffed behind me, which made keeping my balance difficult. Bryn left and came back a few minutes later with a tray of ice cubes, a metal clip, a dildo, and a bottle of lube. She clipped my collar to the top of the cage, which took some of the pressure off my stomach and knees and transferred it to my neck.

She put on a plastic glove, lubed up her finger and started pressing against my asshole while moving her finger in small circles.

"I really want this to work, Taylor. I don't want to have to spend all day punishing you."

She pushed harder and the tip of her finger popped inside of me. She kept up the pressure.

"Relax your butt muscles. I want us to get to the point where we can have fun together."

Her finger went deeper inside me, and she started to push it in and out.

"But we can't have fun together until you accept what you are and who makes the decisions, and I mean all the decisions. You haven't done that."

She removed her finger and pressed the dildo against my asshole.

"You keep thinking that this is a game. Deep breath in. But it's not."

I breathed in and she pushed the dildo up inside me. I grunted.

"This is the widest part. Hang with it. We're not equals, Taylor. You're my slave. You do as I say and then you thank me for it afterwards. You don't think about whether you like it or not, or whether it's humiliating or not: you just do it."

The widest part felt like it was forearm width, though I knew from seeing it that the dildo wasn't much more than two fingers. It finally passed the excruciating part and thinned. My sphincter cinched around it.

"Now. While you're here, I want you to reflect on your shitty attitude and how all of your problems could be solved if you just stopped being such a control freak. You're my slave, and this will all get easier when you start acting like it."

She closed the cage door and locked it. Then she picked up the tray of ice cubes and emptied them on the top of the wire cage.

"Oh, I almost forgot!"

She left the room and went downstairs. A few of the ice cubes started to drip; the freezing cold water felt like little knives pricking my skin.

Bryn came back holding a kitchen timer. She wound it to 40 minutes and placed it in front of the cage, facing me.

"Think about it, Taylor. I have films of you masturbating and pictures of you sucking a cock, plus you sent me threatening emails. What are you going to do?"

She left.

More cubes started dripping. I couldn't move to avoid them since my neck was attached to the top of the cage. I looked at the timer. Not even a minute had gone by. Shit. I closed my eyes and tried to meditate. The timer was the old-fashioned kind which made a ticking noise that was impossible to ignore. Plus my ass felt like it was filled with a tennis ball can.

I thought about some of my favorite songs and sung them. I shouldn't have, but I thought again about when Bryn asked me to use my shower – when she got on my email and installed the cameras in my room – and this time I said no. I thought about my classes and the papers I would write. All the while the ice kept dripping, sending me into involuntary spasms as my body jerked with each drip. The inside of my ass hurt and my ass cheeks were sore. The beatings Bryn had given me were adding up, and my ass felt bruised. I sung my favorite song again, then a different song. I tried not to think about how much time was left. I was bored. I tried to meditate a little more. Finally, I checked on the time.

Six minutes had gone by.

I knelt in the cage as time painfully, agonizingly ticked on. After a little while the ice stopped dripping. I didn't look at the timer.

I heard Bryn's feet climb the stairs. I looked up as she came into the room holding another tray of ice. She dumped it on top of the cage and walked out without saying a word.

There were 16 minutes left.

Anyone who says time is constant has never been locked in a cage with ice cubes slowly dripping on his back and a dildo shoved in his ass. I've had entire months fly by quicker. The kitchen timer was a nice touch, and I had to admire Bryn's creativity. The constant ticking never let me forget where I was or how slow time progressed. When the kitchen timer finally dinged, I was exhausted. Again I felt that it would be better just to do what Bryn wanted until she got bored and let me go. I'd eat all my food off her feet if it meant I didn't have to go through this cage punishment again.

Bryn came upstairs and stood in front of the cage looking down at me with her arms crossed. I peered up at her then dropped my gaze to the ground. I was exhausted physically and mentally. She walked around to unlock the cage, then pulled the dildo out of my butt and unhooked my collar. She guided me out of the cage and I dove toward her feet.

"Thank you, Master. Thank you for punishing me and thank you for releasing me from the cage."
She knelt down and took my face in her hands. She stared into my eyes, then kissed me slowly on the forehead.
"I brought your clothes from yesterday. Get dressed and come downstairs."

I got dressed. Could it really only be 24 hours since I got here? It seemed like so much longer. I hurried downstairs and kissed Bryn's feet.

"Kneel."

I quickly sat back on my heels with my chest raised. Bryn reached behind me and undid my collar.

"Go to the gym."
"What? I mean, what Master?"

"Go to your house and get your workout clothes, then go to the gym. Shower afterwards, cold water only. Be back here by 7."

I couldn't believe it. My body felt so cramped and uncomfortable; a hard workout would really do me well. I stuttered a quick "thank you Master" and turned towards the door. Suddenly I realized what I forgot and quickly sank to my knees and kissed Bryn's feet again.

"Thank you Master."
"You're welcome slave, now get going."

My legs were still pretty cramped from the cage, but as I walked to my house they woke up. I quickly got my things and jogged to the gym. There I was all business. All of my frustration and anger and sadness I took out on the weights. I ran five miles on the treadmill. I stretched and looked at my watch. I had time, but I couldn't risk being late. I knew this must be a test, and who knows what failing it would mean. I hustled to the shower and turned it on full blast. I was about to step into the hot water when I remembered Bryn's instruction, "cold water only."

How would she know? Something told me she would know if I took a hot shower. I hesitated. I wanted a hot shower so badly for my sore muscles. But she'd know. She'd definitely know. I sighed and turned the water to cold, then got in and quickly cleaned myself. I hustled back to Bryn's, arriving with eight minutes to spare. I waited on her porch until 6:59, then rang the doorbell.

Bryn came to the door wearing a beautiful, low cut midnight blue dress. She had put on just a bit of makeup, and her hair fell gently over her shoulders. The house smelled great, and the lights were low. I fell to my knees and kissed her feet. She reattached my collar.

"Come slave. I've made us dinner."

I was shocked, and I half-expected it to be a joke or for her to put me into a butler's uniform and serve her. But she had made us a chicken dinner with coconut rice and zucchini. We even had a little wine. She asked me about my research and what I was working on. She was attentive and asked great questions, and she had interesting ideas of her own. We talked about her own work and I helped clear up a few misconceptions that would have cost her a lot of time and effort. After the discomfort of the past 24 hours, it felt strange to just sit and talk to her. I had worked up a lot of anger, but it was hard to hold on to it as we sat and talked and she made witty and funny remarks. I wanted to believe we had turned some kind of corner, but the collar around my neck never let me.

"Clear the table and wash the dishes, slave. Then strip and go to the computer room."

I met her in the computer room, where she had me kneel on the floor and watch another video. This one was titled "Ejaculation Domination," and it was about cum control and orgasm without ejaculation.

"Slave, one day we might have sex. If that happens, you better be good, which means lasting long. I know you probably think you're great at sex – you're a cocky shit about most things – but I bet you wouldn't last three minutes with me. So you're going to get good at cum control just like you're getting good at pussy eating. Watch, learn, then meet me in the living room."

I had expected another video with poor lighting and some dude with a mustache, but it was actually a well-done video with interesting ideas and good practice. I wish I'd gotten a hold of this in high school. There were exercises to do for this as well.

When I finished, I found Bryn sitting on a towel on her living room sofa. There was a folded yoga mat beneath her feet. She looked at me seriously.

"Kneel on the yoga mat."

I looked up as Bryn lifted her dress above her waist. She leaned forward and took my chin in her hand.

"You haven't earned my pussy yet, slave. But I'm going to let you watch as I masturbate. Lean forward and put your chin on the edge of the couch."

I felt my cock stir and press against its plastic cage. I could hear Bryn breathing heavily as she grabbed onto the back of my head and moved her left hand slowly down to her underwear. She rubbed her crotch slowly in a circle.

"Look at me."

I stared into her eyes. Her breathing picked up as her mouth fell open slightly. I could smell her arousal.

"Pull my underwear down."

I slid Bryn's panties down to her feet and held them as she stepped her feet clear. I put my face back onto the edge of the couch and watch up close as she alternated between softly stroking her clit and sticking her fingers inside herself.

"Look at me slave. Don't take your eyes off me."

She threw her head back and moaned as she pulled my hair. Her hips bucked as her chest rose and fell with her quick, sharp breaths.

"Oh . . . fuck! Look at me. Don't stop looking into my eyes. Oh . . . GOD! FUCK!!!" She came then, hard, then pushed me away and curled over onto her side and rubbed her legs together.

"Slave that was good! Get me a glass of water with two ice cubes. I want us to watch a movie together."

When I returned, I learned that watching a movie with Bryn meant massaging her feet and licking her ass as she watched Miller's Crossing, a Coen brothers movie I'd seen about a dozen times. When it was finished, she stood and reattached the leash to my collar. She led me upstairs.

"Slave, you can now ask me questions. Remember last night, though. Unless you liked the feeling of sports rub on the head of your dick, I'd advise you to be more careful."

I kissed her feet and sat back on my heels. I kept my mouth shut.

"No questions?"

I shook my head,

"No, Master."
"You can call me Bryn during our Q and A. Surely you must have one."
"No, Bryn."

"I'm not a mind reader, Taylor. So here's some advice. think of at least one question for me. Otherwise I might think you don't appreciate this kindness I'm showing you. That would make me angry and then I'd have to probably go get that lollipop crop and work out that anger on your ass."

"I do have a question, now that you put it that way."
"I thought you might."
"Do you have to beat me so much?"
"I beat you exactly as much as you deserve. If you were quicker and better behaved, I'd beat you less. But since you're stubborn and seem committed to being as dense as possible where your responsibilities to me are concerned, I have to punish you. Otherwise, I'm not being a good Master, and I won't do that."

She took my chin in her hand.

"You do what I say. You don't question my commands; you don't think about whether you want to do them; you just obey. Do you think you're at that point yet?"

"No. I don't."

"Me neither. You still act like we're equals, which we're obviously not, or you wouldn't be sitting on my floor naked except for the collar I put on you, and your dick wouldn't be locked in a cage."

She paused to let that sink in.

"You're my slave, and you're going to act like it. If that means I have to beat your ass raw every two hours, I'll do it. So to answer your question, yes, the beatings will continue . . . until morale improves."

She laughed at her joke. Pretty fucking funny.

"Ok, slave. Q and A is over. Brush your teeth and go the bathroom. You're going back in the cage."

I looked at her pleadingly. I had thought our dinner meant something. I had thought we had made at least a little progress.

"Don't give me those puppy dog eyes. You can't possibly think you've earned the bed! How many times did I have to punish you today? Do better tomorrow and maybe you won't have to sleep in the cage three nights in a row . . . maybe."

I brushed my teeth and went to the bathroom. Afterwards I crawled into the cage and Bryn closed and locked the door. She crouched down.

"Slave, I know you took a cold shower at the gym and I'm pleased. You're obeying me quicker now, and that's good. Now go to sleep. You've got a big day ahead of you."

I curled into a ball and thought, for the thousandth time in the last 30 hours, how different my life would be if I hadn't let Bryn use my shower. After a little while, I fell asleep.

Chapter 8

It was another rough night of sleep. I woke up several times with stabbing pains in my groin from my chastity belt. Apparently my dick had yet to learn that night erections were forbidden. My legs and back were cramped and stiff from being curled up all night. Bryn had heavy curtains over the windows, so I couldn't tell within five hours what time it was. And of course I had to piss. I tossed and turned as much as I could until I heard the door open.

"Get up." Bryn unlocked my cage. I crawled out and she unhooked my collar. "Bathroom, teeth, cold shower, shave. You have 10 minutes."

I moved quickly to the bathroom and was downstairs kissing her feet in eight minutes.

"Down."

I pressed my forehead against the floor and waited while she walked around me.

"Present."

I lifted my head up.

"Kneel."

This continued for around five minutes, until Bryn was satisfied I hadn't forgotten the commands she'd beaten into me yesterday morning. She then ordered me to make breakfast: eggs, toast and turkey bacon on a plate at the table for her and oatmeal in a bowl on the floor for me.

When Bryn had finished and I had washed her dishes, she let me eat. I had to keep my hands behind my back, which meant I fell over into my food a number of times, all to Bryn's enjoyment. At one point, as I was eating, I felt Bryn's foot on the back of my head. She pressed down, mashing my face into the oatmeal, laughing as she did so, the fucking bitch.

Afterwards she forbade me from washing my face, so I had crusted oatmeal on my face for the rest of the morning. She sent me to the computer room to watch another video on oral sex, then back to the living room.

"Slave, you're going to clean the kitchen and living room this morning while I meet a friend for coffee. I want everything spotless when I return."

"Yes, Master."

"Oh, and I have a present for you to wear while you clean. It's on the sink in the bathroom. Bring everything to me."

I wondered what she could have for me, a ball gag? a hair-shirt? On the sink I saw a butt-plug, a bottle of lube and a rubber glove. Shit.

"Over my knee, slave."

My cock jumped and pressed against its cage at the idea of laying across her lap. Memories of Natalie spanking me came flooding back, and I was momentarily lost. My mouth felt dry.

"Slave? What's wrong?"

"Nothing, Master."
"Slave. Tell me."
"I just . . . got a little dizzy."

Bryn studied my face. I knew she saw something, but she let it go and pulled me over her knees. She opened her legs and trapped my cock between her thighs. My heart started beating faster.

Bryn put on the rubber glove and lubed up her finger, then started pushed her finger in slow circles around my asshole. I concentrated on the feeling and tried to gather myself. I had nearly lost it when Bryn put me over her lap, and I knew I couldn't tell her about Natalie. She would use it as proof that I wanted to be a slave.

"Something's weird with you, slave."
"I'm sorry Master. I feel out of it, that's all."

Bryn pushed her finger inside of me and I groaned. She moved it in and out slowly. I jerked. It felt embarrassingly good. Bryn finger-fucked me for a minute before removing her finger and pushing the butt-plug inside of me. It went in somewhat easily until it got to the thick middle. I couldn't believe something that size could feel like someone's forearm. I groaned, but I was grateful for the pain for bringing me back to the present. Bryn pushed the plug past it's thickest point and my asshole relaxed a small bit.

"Kitchen, then the living room. I haven't had to beat you today, slave. Don't make me start. Nod yes."

I nodded, then leaned forward and kissed her feet.
"Thank you Master."

She got up wordlessly and walked upstairs. When I tried to stand I learned that having a butt-plug inside of you made standing straight difficult. It also made walking difficult. I shuffled - bent over around 45 degrees at the waist - to get the cleaning materials. I heard the shower running. I still felt odd from being pulled over Bryn's lap. It had felt like I was going to faint. As I was cleaning the countertops in the kitchen, Bryn came in dressed casually in tan pants and a dark blue t-shirt. The clothes seemed like they were tailored specifically for her body. I'm not sure how she managed to make such everyday clothes look so good, but she did, and I felt a surge of guilt because it made me happy to kneel and kiss her feet. I reminded myself that I was just pretending until I got my chance to break free of Bryn's blackmail.

Again, I did a very thorough job of cleaning the kitchen and the living room. I found that if I concentrated on the cleaning, I could better ignore the plug in my ass and the dried oatmeal on my face. Plus, I had seen what Bryn could do when she was upset with me. I wasn't interested in satisfying her sadism any more than I'd already done.

I finished before Bryn came back from brunch, so I went back over the kitchen and living room a second time. I was putting away the cleaning supplies when she walked in. I hustled over to her and kissed her feet.

"Good slave. Let's see how you did." She walked around the living room, running her fingers over all the surfaces to see how well I had dusted. She looked in the refrigerator under the condiments to see if I had cleaned the shelves. I had. I thought I detected a hint of displeasure in her face that she wouldn't be able to carry out some terrible punishment on me.

"Very impressive, slave. I think I'm going to reward you. Crawl upstairs and wash your face, then lie face up on the bed in your bedroom. There are cuffs on each post. Lock your ankles and your right wrist."

It felt good to wash my face. In my "bedroom," I cuffed myself to the bed and waited. My dick seemed to think it was going to get released, because it pushed against its cage trying to get hard. After a few minutes I heard Bryn walk up the steps and enter the room. She was pulling on a rubber glove as she spoke.

"I'm very proud of you, Taylor. You're proving that you might just have some value."

She leaned over and cuffed my left wrist.

"Admittedly, I was hoping to get to punish you. But you're such a good little maid that I have no choice but to reward you. Lift your butt."

She placed a pillow underneath me and then sat on the bed. She unclasped her necklace, on the end of which was the key to my chastity belt. She unlocked and removed it, and huge wave of relief washed over me. My dick got hard right away. Bryn gave my balls a quick squeeze, then grabbed the end of the butt-plug. But instead of pulling it out, she pushed it in. She slowly pulled it out just a little, just until I felt the wide middle push against my sphincter, then pushed it in. She pulled it out and pushed it in again. And then again.

"Your dick is very hard, slave. You must like this."

"No Master."
She mocked my voice "No, Master, my dick just turns super hard when you fuck me with the butt-plug, but I don't like it."

I didn't respond.

"Don't get all sulky, little one. It's ok to like a plug in your ass. It doesn't mean you're gay. Deep breath in."

She pulled the plug out of me. I was able to relax my muscles more, so it hurt less coming out this time. Bryn walked out of the room and came back a moment later with a small tin box.

"I have some gifts for you, slave."

She sat back on the bed and smiled at me. I didn't smile back. I had a feeling these weren't going to be the kind of gifts I wanted. Bryn grabbed my balls and squeezed hard.

"Unhhh!!"
"Let's try this again. I have some gifts for you, slave."
"Ahhh, thank you Master."
"Aren't you curious what they are?"
"What are they Master?"

She released my balls.

"Better."

She ran her hand around my stomach and up to my right nipple. She drew small circles around it with the tip of her index finger. She pinched it lightly, then leaned over a blew on it. It felt wonderful. She pulled out a metal clothespin, pinched the bottom and clamped it over my now erect nipple.

"Oh come on, it doesn't hurt that bad. From what I've heard it even feels good. Right, slave!"
"Yes Master!"

She repeated the process with my left nipple. Then she straddled my stomach and leaned over and kissed me. Her hair fell over and tickled my cheeks.

"Let me guess," she said. "You're rock hard right now."

She reached back to confirm it.

"I've known guys who were into this stuff before, slave, but no one who loved it as much as you did. What do you think about that?"
"I don't, Master."
"You don't what?"
"I don't think I love it."

She brought her hands to the tips of the clothespins and squeezed. I gasped.

"After all I've done to you: all the humiliation and pain, the emotional distress, all the chores and beatings, and your dick still gets hard as a rock whenever I touch you. That means one of two things: either your dick is controlled by someone else, or you get off on being my slave but just don't want to admit it up here."

She tapped her finger against my forehead.

"Don't pout. You're not the first guy to love being a slave. Here, I'll make it feel good."

She turned around and traced her fingers up and down my cock. I sank back and gave in to the feeling. Fighting it wasn't going to do any good and would just give her more ammo. Bryn poured lube into her hand and started stroking me slowly.

"Who owns you slave?" She whispered.
"Ohhhh, you do, Master."
"Who do you want to control you, my sweet slave?"
"You Master."
"Anyone else?"
"No, Master, just you."
"Just me what?"
"Just you controlling me, Master."
"That's right slave."

I was going to cum. I could feel it building. It would just take a few more strokes.

Bryn took her hand off my cock.

"Not so fast. We've got a full afternoon ahead of us."

She turned around and removed the clothespins from my nipples. Pain shot through my chest.

"Hurts coming off, huh?"

Bryn smiled. She turned around.

"Your dick is still hard."
"Yes, Master."
"How close were you to cumming a moment ago?"
"Very close, Master."

"And do you know what would have happened if you'd cum without permission?"
"Something bad, Master."
"That's right, so shouldn't you be thanking me for not making you cum?"
"Thank you, Master."

She tilted her head.

"I don't think you meant that."

She picked up the clothespins and reapplied them. I bucked as pain tore through my chest again. She turned around and stuck her ass in my face.

"Kiss my ass. Don't lick it. Just kisses."

I did as she asked while she took my dick in her hand again. I had calmed down, and my dick was only half-erect, but it grew to full mast after just a few strokes. Bryn worked my dick expertly: she gave a couple strokes, then waited, then lightly ran the tips of her fingers up my shaft until I felt ready to burst, only to pull her hand away at the last moment. When I calmed down she started all over again. She knew exactly when to stop to keep me from spilling over. I lay my head back against the pillow and moaned. Bryn turned and lay next to me. She put her lips near my ear as she kept her right hand lightly stroking my cock.

"Slave, do you want to cum."
"Oh, Master, please! Please may I cum?"

She licked my ear and whispered:

"No."

She giggled as I let out an involuntary groan. She straddled my chest and took my face in her hands.

"Two days slave. It hasn't even been two whole days! You may have to go two weeks before you cum again."

I thought I might cry. Bryn reached down and took off the clothespins. It hurt, but I didn't respond to it. Bryn got down off the bed. She held my chin in her hand and leaned forward to kiss me, pushing her tongue into my mouth. I pushed my tongue back against hers, but she pulled away.

"What do you say, slave?"
"Thank you Master."
"Thank you for what?"
"I'm not sure, Master."
"How about thank you for my nice reward, Master."
"Thank you for my nice reward, Master."
"You're welcome, slave."

Bryn left the room, and I lay back against the pillow. My breath was still a little ragged, and my dick still felt like a few good hard strokes would take me over the edge. But those strokes weren't coming. I wanted to feel Bryn's body against mine, to feel her hands on my face. I closed my eyes and tried and failed not to think about her.

Chapter 9

Bryn came back into the room after about half an hour. My dick started to rise, until she covered it with a bag of ice. I managed not to scream this time. I was soon locked back into my chastity cage and kissing her feet as she sat on the bed.

"Kneel."

She took my face in her hands.

"Would you like to ask me something, slave?"
"Yes, Master."
"You may."
"Master, I have work to do before my classes tomorrow. I also have to work on a few papers. May I have some time to do that?"
"I thought you'd ask me that. Yes. We just have one more thing to do and then you can go home. But there are some rules you must follow."
"Yes Master."
"First, you don't take hot showers. You only take cold showers. You haven't earned a hot shower yet. Second, you cannot sleep in your bed. You can sleep on a couch or on a blow-up mattress if you have one, but that bed in your house is now mine and I'll decide when you can sleep there. Third, you have homework. You're to write a brief dedication to me that you will read every morning and every night. Something like, "I am your slave, and your happiness is my first responsibility. I live to serve you and tend to your every need." You get the idea. Fourth, I will have further instructions for you. I'm guessing you shut your phone off when you work? You seem the type."
"Yes, Master. I do."

"Check your email every hour on the hour. Understand all those rules? Nod yes."

I nodded.

"Good boy." She patted my head, then attached the leash to my collar. "Crawl after me downstairs."

When we got to the first floor, Bryn kept walking in the direction of the basement. I followed her down to the basement with dread in stomach.

"Up over the bench."

Bryn cuffed me face down over the spanking bench then walked to the wall and pulled down leather crop.

"I'm trusting you, Taylor. You're getting to go home and work unsupervised. Most slaves don't get that."
"Thank you, Master."
"But I want to give you something to remember our time together this weekend and reinforce our relationship."

She walked around me, dragging the tip of the crop down my spine, then set it down. She rubbed her hand in a circle over my ass, then gave me some light spanks.

"You may be thinking -"

She gave me three quick, medium-strength spanks.

"What have I done? Why am I getting punished?"
"Yes, Master."

SPANK! SPANK! SPANK!

"Am I warming you up, slave?"
"Yes, Master."
"So is this punishment?"
"No, Master, it's discipline."
"Correct, slave."

SPANK! SPANK! SPANK!

"And when can I discipline you?"
"Whenever you want, Master."
"Good slave."

She picked up the crop and gave me twenty-seven increasingly hard smacks. Then she bent down and grabbed my testicles.

"Your balls seem full, slave. Are they sensitive?"
"Very much so, Master."
"Does it hurt when I squeeze them?" She squeezed gently.
"Yes Master!"
"If I squeeze harder does it hurt more or less?" She squeezed hard.
"More Master!! More!"
“Really?”
“Wha-, yes, really! Master!”
"That was a joke, slave. Lighten up."

She released my balls and uncuffed me from the bench.

"Your clothes are in the cupboard at the back of this room. Meet me in the living room when you're dressed."

It felt strange to put on the clothes I'd been wearing Friday. It seemed like a different person had been wearing them then. I couldn't figure out the emotions going through me. I was still angry with Bryn, but there were other thoughts warring with my desire for revenge. I've always been pretty clear about what I think; I'm an uncomplicated guy, I guess. I didn't feel like trying to psychoanalyze myself. Besides, Bryn had already shown she wasn't the most patient person in the world.

She was sitting on the couch with her back straight. She looked regal. I knelt before her and kissed her feet. She reached down and lifted my chin up with her finger. I looked into her eyes.

"When you get home, you may have certain ideas about what happened the last two days. You may think you should do something stupid. Trust me, you don't want to do that. I like you, Taylor, but that won't stop me from hurting you. Don't speak. Just nod."

I nodded. Bryn caressed my cheek.

"I like you, Taylor. I want us to both be happy." She kissed me, deeply, fully. And I kissed her back. "What are your four rules?"

"Cold showers. No sleeping on the bed. Write a short dedication to you. Check my email on the hour."
"Good slave."

She reached around and unhooked my collar. She held my chin.

"You still have a ways to go, but you've come a long way in the last 48 hours. I'm proud of you, Taylor."

I felt a little pride in my chest, then guilt and shame for feeling that pride.

"Thank you, Master."
"At school, you can call me Bryn."
"Thank you, Master."
"Now go."

I gave her feet two more kisses, then left.

As I walked home, I felt like I should assess what I was feeling and why her praise of me being a good slave felt good, but I didn't want to. It had been a humiliating, painful and frightening two days. And I was still under Bryn's thumb. She could ruin my career, and she seemed set on making me her slave. And yet, as I walked, my thoughts strayed to when she held my face in her hands and kissed me, and – embarrassingly – when I kissed her feet and licked her asshole. I had work to do, and untangling a bunch of crazy feelings wouldn't do any good.

At home I drank two big glasses of water, then fixed myself a steak and some vegetables. I was starving. I checked my email at 6. There were new messages – I hadn't checked my email since Friday afternoon – but none from Bryn. I started working on my book. I wanted something to take up all my attention, and the book was perfect. I set my phone to airplane mode and set the alarm for 6:59. In what seemed like no time at all, it went off. I checked my email. No messages. I set the alarm again and got back to work. No messages at 8 or 9, either.

As I worked, my view towards Bryn and her hold on me changed. Now that I was fully fed and hydrated I could think clearly. I couldn't believe I'd done the things I did. Why didn't I walk out on Friday night and call her bluff?

And I called her "Master"?!?! What the hell was wrong with me?! I flushed red thinking of what she'd done, at what I'd done. Anger ran through me. Things would change now.

At 10, there was an email from Bryn:

> *Taylor,*
> *Most likely, you're battling with your new role in life and the events of this weekend. You may even have promised yourself that things were going to be different. This is a natural step on your path to accepting yourself as my slave and the last throes of your ego trying to keep you in your previous state of unrealized dissatisfaction.*
>
> *Just in case you're thinking of doing something stupid, though, click on the following link.*
>
> *-Master*

The link took me to Taylorclark.com. The home page had a large gif of me masturbating, right before I came, looking completely insane. Underneath it read:

Professor Taylor Clark of Clareville University is available for sex shows in your area. Nothing is too degrading or off-limits. His specialties include:
Humiliation and Role-Play
Cocksucking
BDSM (submissive only)
Light Cleaning

Somewhat Intellectual Discourse

Rates are very cheap. Call any time!

There were some pictures at the bottom of me sucking the rubber dildo. There were also pictures of me in the cage and one of me asleep tied spread-eagle to the bed.

I picked up an old clock next to my computer and smashed it on the ground. I wanted to kill her. I would go over there, strangle her and hide the body.

But even through my rage, I knew I wasn't going to do that. There was way too much evidence pointing at me, and I'd spend my life behind bars. But more than that – and this was difficult to admit – I didn't want to hurt Bryn. When I pictured hurting her, which I'd done a lot over the weekend, I felt bad. It just felt wrong.

She didn't answer when I called, but twenty seconds later she sent a text:
"At 10:30, turn on Skype and call me."

After pacing the house for half an hour, I called:

"Hello slave."
"Hello Master."
"You look upset, slave. You don't like your website?"
"No, Master, I don't."
"I'm not sure I like your tone, slave. That website is private, but it doesn't have to be."
"Master, that would ruin me. I'd have nothing left to live for after that."
"Oh, slave, don't be so melodramatic."

I didn't answer. If she ruined me, I'd have no reason to be her slave any longer. It was a worse trade for me, obviously, which was why she had such control over me. But I felt she was bluffing and wouldn't make the website public unless I did something major.

"Why, Master?"
"Why the reminder? Were you thinking of rebelling against me."
"I was working, Master."
"Slave, I can tell your lying, even through the computer."
"Master, I was enjoying being able to work on my paper and not get beaten or have to clean or be naked all the time. I need some time to think of my work. You know how it is when writing a paper, the ideas you have form in your head during the day and–"
"Stop talking."

I stopped.

"I asked if you were thinking of rebelling against me. Yes or no?"
"Yes . . . Master."
"And are you still thinking of rebelling against me?"

I didn't want to admit it, but since she seemed to know when I was lying anyway,

"No, Master."
"So the website was necessary, wouldn't you say, slave?"
"Yes, Master."
"Stand up and take off all your clothes"

I did.

"Have you done your homework yet?"
"No Master, I was working on my book."
"This whole time?"
"I ate dinner first, then yes. Since 6."
"Very good, slave. I like that you're working hard. You need to work on my dedication now. You're to email me the dedication before 11:30pm, then I want you in bed, well, not in a *bed*, but going to sleep by midnight. You have to be over here by 7:30 tomorrow morning. And I emailed you a link to a video. Watch it before bed. Nod yes."

I nodded.

"Good night slave."
"Good night Master."

The video was "How to Give a Mind-Blowing Foot Massage." After five minutes it started to get technical, so I jotted down notes. No doubt there'd be a practical test the next day. I worked on Bryn's dedication and emailed it to her before climbing on the couch at 12. It wasn't my bed, but compared to the cage I'd slept in the last two nights, it was wonderful. I was asleep in less than a minute.

Chapter 10

In the morning I had a blissful moment of not knowing why I was sleeping on the couch. Why wasn't I in bed? And then I remembered and all the memories from the weekend came flooding into my brain. I took a cold shower, ate breakfast and headed to Bryn's. She answered the door in her robe. I stepped inside and dropped to my knees to kiss her feet.

"Good slave. Take your clothes off and come into the living room."

I knelt between Bryn's feet as she sat on the couch. Her legs were open and I could see her pubic hair through her black lace underwear.

"Slave, what time do you have to be in your office?"
"9:30."
"9:30 what?!"
"9:30 Master. I'm sorry Master, I forgot."
"Slave, there's a paddle on the kitchen table. Crawl over and get it."

Shit. I crawled into the kitchen, got the paddle and carried it out to her.

"Present."

I stayed on all fours. Bryn walked to my side and put her foot in between my hands.

"Press your lips against my foot. Do NOT break contact with my foot."

WHAP! WHAP! WHAP!

"Who am I!"
"You're my Master!" I spoke into her foot.

WHAP! WHAP! WHAP!

"Are you going to forget that?"
"No Master!"

WHAP! WHAP! WHAP!

"What time do you have to be in your office?"
"9:30 Master."
"Not 11? Your first class is at 11:30."
"No, Master. I have work to do before my classes."
"You couldn't do that last night?"
"No Master, I didn't have time."
"Kneel."

I sat on my heels as Bryn sat down on the couch.

"I read your dedication, slave. It was fair, at best."
"I'm sorry, Master."
"It felt half-hearted. Sometimes I wonder why you volunteered to be my slave in the first place."

I glanced quickly at her face. She ran her hand along my cheek.

"I know, I know. You think I'm blackmailing you. But really, Taylor, you all but volunteered."

She wanted to get a rise out of me, and she was succeeding. But I kept quiet.

"I rewrote it." She handed me a sheet of paper. "Read it out loud."

"You are my Master and I submit to you. My purpose is to serve you and make you happy. I will obey your commands immediately and without question. I worship, obey and fear you. By accepting your will as my own, I am a better and more content person. Without you I am lost and unhappy. Please accept me as your slave, and do with me as you will."

"I accept! Now give me a foot massage, slave. Ten minutes per foot. Show me you learned something from the video so I don't have to spend the next hour and a half beating you."

I massaged her feet. I remembered the video and did – in my opinion – a good job.

"Mmmm, slave. That was nice. Now I'm turned on." She opened her robe and reached down into her underwear. When she brought her finger out, it was wet. She held it out to me.

"Lick."

I tasted her juices.

"Now slave, I'm going to let you lick my pussy, but just one lick, from the bottom to the top. No more. Nod yes."

I nodded. She lifted her butt and pushed her underwear down to the floor. Then she grabbed my head and pulled my face towards her. I started at the base of her vagina and ran my tongue as slowly as I could towards the top. Bryn inhaled sharply and pushed my head back.

"Oh, slave, that was wonderful. That's going to be so nice when you get to really eat me out."
"Thank you Master."
"Now get up on the couch on your back, you're going to lick my asshole while I get myself off."

It didn't take long for Bryn to orgasm. Afterwards she sent me to the kitchen to make her breakfast: an omelette with mushrooms, onions and dill and a side of broccoli. I served her, then washed the dishes.

"Slave. At 1pm I'm done with my first class, just like you are. I'll meet you in the staff parking lot at 1:15 and you'll drive me home. Then I have your 4pm seminar, so you'll drive me to class at 3:30. Nod yes."

I nodded.

"Now go to class. Don't eat lunch today, and you can drink one glass of water before your 11:30 class and one before your 4pm seminar. On the table in the front hall there's a list of things I need you to buy for me: groceries and some odds and ends. Have them for me by 3:30. Now go."

I kissed her feet and walked towards the door, but Bryn stopped me and had me kneel in front of her.

"Here's something to remember me today."

She reached into her underwear and pushed her finger inside of her. Then she smeared it under my nose.

"Don't wash that off. Now be good, and maybe I'll take you out of your cage later tonight." She fingered my chastity belt key at the end of her necklace. I gave her feet a couple more kisses and left.

At work I alternated between concentrating on my work and smelling Bryn's scent. I also went for short periods of time without noticing my chastity cage. I had checked in the mirror from as many angles as possible to see if the cage was noticeable through my pants. Even though it wasn't, I wore a jacket that covered my groin and kept it on all day.

I also had a brief moment of panic that my students would somehow know what I'd done this weekend. I knew it was irrational, but I was certain they'd be able to tell all the fucked up things Bryn had me do.

When my first class started, though, I sunk into a familiar rhythm of teaching and it was clear that no one knew that the man standing before them had just hours earlier kissed the feet of one of their classmates and called her "Master." Time flew by, and the class was completely engaged. It felt good.

I waited for Bryn in the parking lot at 1:15. She showed at 1:30 without an explanation or apology. She barely looked at me as she got into the car and said "Let's go." After a minute of silence she turned to me:

"Could they tell?"
"Could who tell?"

"Sorry, could who tell, Master?"
"You know exactly what I mean."
"No, they couldn't."
"Just pull up in front of my house and let me out. You have shopping to do."

Bryn's shopping list forced me to go to four different stores. I had thought she might try to humiliate me by making me buy embarrassing items, but other than an enema kit, everything was normal. I found everything but one item – a particular type of shampoo – but I had the store special order it for me.

Back at Bryn's house, I took off my clothes and made her lunch. I knelt at her feet. Every once in a while she dropped a piece of food onto the floor and ordered me to eat it keeping my hands behind my back. When she was done, she put her plate onto the floor and I licked the crumbs off of it.

After washing the dishes, I knelt at her feet.
"Master, may I talk about something with you?"
"Is it about our class at 4?"
"Yes Master."
"Go ahead."
"I'm worried that . . . I'm hoping that-"
"You're worried I might embarrass you? You think I might call you slave or demand you kiss my feet in front of everyone?"
"No, Master. Well, yes Master. I am afraid of that. I just, I know it's different here and-"
"Slave. During class, you are Dr. Clark and I'm Bryn. If I say something wrong, you can tell me I'm wrong. I'm not going to humiliate you unless I have to. And I think it's clear that you're going to obey me here, so I don't have to embarrass you over there. Relax slave. I'll be just another one of the starstruck coeds who think you're dreamy."
"Thank you Master."

"The only difference is that tonight, the rest of the girls will do homework and dream about you, but I'll have you licking my pussy."

I looked up at her.

"That's right, slave. Tonight you get to taste my pussy . . . if you're good."
"Thank you Master."

She looked down at her feet, and I kissed them. I kept kissing them until it was time to go to class.

In our seminar, I lectured and tried as hard as I could not to look at Bryn. I succeeded somewhat. I didn't embarrass myself or gawk at her, but as I lectured, Bryn fingered the key to my chastity belt that was on her necklace. It was an effective reminder and a bit distracting. It took awhile, but the class finally found it's rhythm, and when it ended I felt like I had cleared some major hurdle.

In my office after class, Bryn came in without knocking. "Not bad, Taylor. Do you feel relieved you made it through our first class without accidentally calling me Master?"
"I do. And thank you for fondling my key while I talked. That was kind of you."
"You're welcome." She smiled.
"Bryn?"
"Yes dear?"
"Can I have a drink of water?"
"No."
"I accept that. But can I ask why?"

Bryn's playful face turned steely.

"Because I said so."
"Ok."
"Anything else you'd like to question?"
"No."
"You can work here until 7, but then you're at my home making me dinner. And we'll see if you still get to taste me."

I must have looked horrorstricken, because Bryn laughed.
"I didn't say you've lost the privilege, but you've irritated me and I'm not sure you get rewarded for that."
"Yes, Bryn."
"I'll see you at 7."

At 7 I was kneeling naked before Bryn as she attached my collar and leash. She was barefoot and wearing her robe. The house smelled like she'd been cooking. I was starving, having obeyed Bryn's order to skip lunch.

"Have you had any more water since this afternoon?"
"No Master."
"Come with me."

In the kitchen, I saw that Bryn had cooked salmon and made a big salad, which waited on the kitchen table. She filled my water dish from the tap and placed it on the floor in front of me. I waited.

"Drink."

I pushed my face into the bowl and slurped at the water while Bryn stood over me. When I was halfway through she pulled me back by the leash.

"Down."

I pressed my forehead to the floor and waited as Bryn grabbed something from the refrigerator.

"Come here, slave."

Bryn sat at the table. By her feet was a plate of what looked like green, slightly watery mashed potatoes.

"We're going to eat dinner together, slave. I'm going to eat salmon and cooked vegetables from a plate at the table, and your going to lick your blended veggies and potatoes off my feet."

She led me under the table, and I watched as she mashed her foot into my dinner. It got everywhere: between her toes, on her heels, up the sides of her foot. She held it up.

"Lick."

I licked her foot clean as she ate her dinner above me. Any ideas I had about our relationship changing went out the window. It was clear that I was still her slave and she was still my master. When she noticed that her foot was clean, she mashed it into the plate again.

"Lick."

I licked again.

"Stop."

She put her foot back into the plate of food and then wiped it down my face.

"Lick."

I licked her foot clean as my food dried on my face. After dinner, I did the dishes and watched another chapter of How to Eat Pussy Like a Champ. This episode was all about the steady drummer theory: once you find something your partner likes, keep doing it. Don't speed up or press harder. Then the short-haired gym-teacher lookalike went in depth about the different parts of the clit and how to find the area that was most sensitive on your partner. I already knew the steady drummer, but the clit specifics were interesting.

As I watched, I couldn't help but think of myself between Bryn's thighs. Her pussy had tasted wonderful this morning, and my dick swelled as much as it could as I thought about Bryn moaning in ecstasy as I slowly explored her with my tongue. Bryn came up behind me as I watched and ran her fingers through my hair.

"Crawl upstairs and wash your face. Then go to your room. I'll be waiting for you."

I hustled up the stairs when I was done. Bryn was sitting on the bed with her robe open. I kissed her feet.

"Grab two pairs of handcuffs. Lock your ankles together and your hands behind your back."

I did. Bryn took off her necklace and unlocked my chastity belt. I sighed with relief as she removed my plastic prison. My dick twitched once or twice, realized it was free, and got hard.

"Take off my underwear with your teeth."

I leaned forward and after a few attempts, got the band of her lace panties between my teeth. At first I pulled back, which just pulled the band forward, then moved from side to side, which did the trick. She lifted her feet and I placed her underwear on the bed by her side. Bryn pointed to her inner thigh.

"Kiss me here."

I gave her inner thigh a slow, passionate kiss. She moved her finger up an inch.

"Here."

Another kiss. She moved her finger an inch below her vagina.

"And here."

She ran her foot over my dick. I lapped her thigh with my tongue before giving it a soft kiss.

"Good slave. Kneel. Your dick is leaking, slave."

It was. Bryn reached behind her and brought out the dildo she had worn on my first night here. The one she'd forced down my throat for more blackmail pictures.

"Remember your friend, slave?"

SLAP!

She slapped my face, hard.

"That was a question!"
"Yes, Master. I remember."

"Did you miss him?"
"No Master."
"That's not very nice, slave. He misses you. Go on, give him a kiss."

She held the dildo up to my lips.

"Three . . . two . . -"

I kissed her dildo.

"Again."

I kissed it again.

"Take it in your mouth, slave. Suck on it."

I opened my mouth and brought it over the dildo. Bryn pushed it slightly into my mouth, then removed it.

"Watch me slave."

She brought the dildo to her pussy and rubbed it back and forth over her opening. She moaned and leaned her hips forward. After a few rubs, she pushed the tip inside her and moved it around. She then pulled it out and held it back to my lips.

"Open."

I opened, and she pushed the dildo inside my mouth.

"Suck."

I sucked her pussy juices off of her make-believe cock. She pulled it away and pushed it back into herself, this time going a little farther in. She lay back and brought her feet up onto the bed.

"Ohhhhh, yeah. That feels so nice, slave. You're going to love when I fuck your ass with this cock."

She pulled it out and sat back up. She brought the dildo back to my lips.

"Open. Suck."

She pushed the dildo farther into my mouth this time, gagging me. She laughed as I coughed. Then she lay back down and pushed the dildo inside her again. This time her hips bucked as she inhaled sharply. She moaned, keeping her mouth open and her eyes closed. She removed the dildo and held the base against her crotch.

"Lean forward, slave. Suck my dick."

She grabbed the back of my head and moved my head forward. I pushed back against her.

"What the fuck are you doing?"
"Sorry Master. It's a reflex."
"Bullshit. What's your problem? You're being a real dud."
"It's nothing, Master."
"I said you'd taste my pussy, slave. You're tasting it, aren't you?"

I didn't say anything. I just stared at her. Fuck her. She grabbed my chin.

"Listen you moody little cunt, we're not boyfriend-girlfriend. You're my slave. You do as I say and you don't ask questions or complain or give me those sad eyes when you don't get everything you want. You get pleasure when you've earned it, and three days of me constantly having to put you in your place hasn't earned you shit. Get downstairs, over the spanking bench. NOW!"

She didn't take off my handcuffs, so I had to hop to the stairs, then sit and schooch down the steps one at a time. I didn't stall, but I didn't hurry, either. I didn't really give a fuck what she did.

In the basement, I leaned over the spanking bench and waited. Bryn stormed in and clamped me to the bench with a series of ropes. She walked to the wall and brought back a leather belt. She folded it over and held the buckle.

WHAP! WHAP! WHAP! WHAP! WHAP! WHAP!

"Happy?"

WHAP! WHAP! WHAP! WHAP! WHAP! WHAP!

"Is this better than tasting my pussy?"

WHAP! WHAP! WHAP! WHAP! WHAP! WHAP!

I was bucking and grunting with each strike. Bryn returned the belt and came back with a cane. My eyes got big.

"What? Now you want to talk?"

Bryn put the cane on my back and went to the cupboard. She came back with a ball gag and strapped it around my head, sticking the ball in my mouth and tightening the straps. She picked up the cane.

SMACK! SMACK SMACK!

I jerked spasmodically with every stroke from her cane. God damn that hurt!

"I was doing you a favor, Taylor. I saw your eyes light up this morning when I said you'd get to taste me. You wanted this, and I wanted it, too! All I wanted was a little fun, first. But you can't think of anything but what you want! It wasn't exactly what you wanted so you sulk and ruin it for me!"

SMACK! SMACK SMACK!

"That was going to be a warm up. Afterwards I was going to let you lick me till your tongue got sore. But you had to be a little brat and now we're both upset. You're a selfish lover, Taylor. I thought you might not be, but you are."

SMACK! SMACK SMACK!

"I wanted this!!" She was screaming now. "I wanted to have a night where I didn't have to treat you like a kid with ADD! But you're too fucking selfish!!"

SMACK! SMACK SMACK!

I was screaming into my gag.

Bryn threw the cane against the wall and stormed out, slamming the door behind her. My ass felt like I'd just been stung by a hive full of wasps. Could Bryn have been right? But she wanted me to suck on a dildo! That's disgusting! But would I have done it if we were lovers? Would it have just been kinky fun? Was I being selfish?

Holy shit, what was I thinking?! I must have Stockholm Syndrome! I was being crazy! I was being blackmailed and tortured and I was worried about being selfish!!

After a long while Bryn came back down and unstrapped me from the table. She pulled me upstairs into the bathroom and pointed to the toilet. I sat. She disappeared from the room, then returned a moment later and uncuffed my hands and feet.

"Teeth, bathroom. You have three minutes."

I met her in my bedroom after. The door to my cage was open and she pointed. I crawled inside.

"Curl up on your side and stick your hands through the bars."

Bryn cuffed my hands to the bars, then walked out without saying a word, turning the light off as she went. I was uncomfortable, but my dick was free from the cage for a night, even though I couldn't touch it. I couldn't figure out if I was being an idiot for not just doing what Bryn said. I wondered how long Bryn would stay angry at me.

Chapter 11

The answer was three days.

For the next three days, Bryn barely spoke to me other than to give me orders. In the morning she put me back into my chastity cage and handed me a schedule for the day.

7 – 8am – shower, shave, make breakfast of oatmeal (cold) and one bowl of water
8 – 9am – watch cum control video, do exercises
9 – 10:30am – go to office, work on book
10:30 – 10:45am – drink a small glass of water and walk outside
10:45 – 11:30am – work on book
11:30 – 1pm – teach class. If no class, work on book.
1 – 3pm – pick up groceries, clean computer room and your bedroom
3 – 4pm – back to office, office hours, grade papers
4 – 4:30pm – write an apology for being a prick or teach seminar
4:30 – 5:30pm – work on your book or teach seminar
5:30 – 7pm – make dinner, eat blended vegetables and potato from a bowl on the floor (no hands) and drink one bowl of water.
7 – 8pm – dust entire house
8pm – in your cage, lights out

It was an unfair schedule, and to make matters worse, Bryn didn't speak to me. She didn't let me touch her. She ate the dinner I prepared for her and then left the kitchen without a word. At night she was waiting for me in the bedroom, but just to open the cage and then close and lock it after me. I thought I'd feel good at not having to kiss her feet or get beaten, but I didn't. I felt guilty, even though it didn't make sense to feel guilty.

The next day Bryn didn't talk to me and didn't let me touch her again. I was in the cage with lights out at 8pm.

Thursday was the same. Still no talking from Bryn. The only difference was that she sent me to my own house at night. She gave me a list of chores to do around my own house and an early bedtime (still no use of my bed).

Friday I awoke and found an email from Bryn telling her to come make her breakfast at 8. I knew I'd have to apologize to her and pretend it was all my fault. It was stupid, but something told me that things would get really bad if I didn't.

Bryn let me in, and as I took off my clothes she sat on the couch with her arms crossed. I went to her and knelt at her feet.

"Don't touch me!"
I waited. She stared at me, still obviously upset. I looked down at her feet until she finally spoke.
"Well?"
"I'm sorry, Bryn– Master. I didn't think I was being selfish. I just – it hasn't even been a week. How can you expect me to be ok with all of this?"

"Of course you didn't think you were being selfish. Selfish people never think they're being selfish; they just are. And I don't expect you to be ok with all of this, but I can expect better from you. Do you think this makes me happy? Do you think I want this?"

"No, Master."

"So what do I do? Just let you be moody and shitty and throw little sulky tantrums whenever you want?"

"No, Master, I'm sorry."

"Of course you're sorry . . . now. But tomorrow I'm going to have to threaten you to think of me first, aren't I?"
"I can do better, Master."
"How am I supposed to believe you?" She shook her head. "I'm upset, and I think I have a right to be. Go make me breakfast."

I made her breakfast and cleaned and drove to my office. I didn't have any classes, so I worked on my book and finished the first chapter. Whatever else I might say about my slavery to Bryn, I was sure getting a lot of work done. I'd been stuck on this chapter for two months. I drove to the flower shop and bought Bryn a dozen flowers. I stopped by a specialty meat store and bought some steaks for dinner, along with beets and kale (her favorites) and a bottle of red wine.

Bryn had left me a set of her keys, and I had a candlelight dinner waiting for her, flowers in a vase on the table, when she got home at seven. She eyed me warily, but I could tell she was impressed by the effort. I served her dinner naked, except for the black bow-tie I'd picked up from home. I stood silently as Bryn ate. After a few minutes she finally cracked a smile.

"That stupid bow-tie. You're such a nerd, Taylor."
"Thank you, Master."
"Are you hungry, slave."
"Yes, Master."

"Kneel."

She cut a piece of steak and held it out on her fork.

"Open."

I opened my mouth and waited.

"Chew."

She fed me half of her steak, then some kale and beets.

"Carry me to your bedroom, slave."

I set her down on the bed, and lay back with her head on my pillows. She took off her necklace and removed my chastity cage.

"Between my legs, slave. Taste me."

I kissed her: light, soft kisses trailing up and around her pussy and close to, but not on, her clit. I then licked her lips slowly, in long strokes: first the right, then the left, then down the center. I paid attention to what made her moan and repeated it. She brought her left hand down to the back of my head and ran her fingernails over my scalp. I put my tongue inside her and she inhaled sharply and arched her back. I pressed my tongue firmly inside of her and licked.

"Ohhh, yesss, slave, like that."

She brought her other hand down to my head and held me firmly as she moved her hips. She let out a deep-throated moan and pressed on my head. I kissed her lips and moved up to her clit. I kissed it softly twice, then brought my tongue down to her opening and back up to her clit. Bryn's breathing picked up. I moved around until I found a very good spot that changed her exhales to moans to cries of ecstasy as I kept softly licking the same spot. Steady fucking drummer.

I brought her to three orgasms that night, and she slept next to me in bed (after cuffing my hands behind my back). She kissed me long and deep, and she stroked my dick, which was as hard as I've ever felt it. She told me that tomorrow I might have a chance to cum, if I were good.

The next morning Bryn had me cook a big breakfast of omelets and spinach and mushrooms for the both of us. She ate hers at the table and I ate mine off a plate on the floor with my hands behind my back. It was better than cold oatmeal. After I cleaned, Bryn told me to go to the gym, which I happily did.

When I came home, Bryn met me in my room and gave me a choice: I could stay locked in the cage with a butt-plug in my ass, or I could take her shopping. I chose the second option.

"Excellent slave. Bend over the bed, I'll be right back."
I looked at her quizzically.
"What? Oh! I didn't say that right. What I meant was you can stay locked in the cage with a butt-plug in your ass, or you can take me shopping with a butt-plug in your ass. Either way, you're getting filled."

She smiled and touched my nose with her finger-tip.

"Yes, Master."

We went to a mall about an hour away: Bryn declared, correctly, that the local mall was shit. I was happy, as there was less chance of running into a Clareville student here.

In the parking lot of the mall we went over a series of speed bumps. I turned and saw that Bryn was smiling, knowing that each bump sent the plug a little deeper inside me. Before we got out of the car, Bryn gave me a list of rules: no speaking unless spoken to, and I was to always walk a few steps behind her, never next to her. Only if we ran into someone I knew or from the University could I speak normally. If we ran into someone she knew she would do the talking for us.

We went first to an Armani store where Bryn looked at the new collections and tried on a few different shirts and skirts. None were up to her liking, though, so we went to an Elie Tahari and she tried on more clothes and bought a sweater. As we left Elie Tahari, I heard a

"Bryn! Sweetie!"

A woman in her late twenties/early thirties came towards us. She had dark brown hair with red streaks and had a thin, toned body. She was stunning, but her face was hard, and unhappy. Something about the way she held herself told me she was a total bitch. I kept these thoughts to myself, obviously.

"Cassandra!" Bryn cried. They hugged and chatted rapidly. I stood behind Bryn for a solid five minutes. Finally, she turned.

"This is Taylor. Taylor, say hello."
"Hi Cassandra."

Cassandra looked me up and down, taking stock, but she didn't return the greeting.

"We miss you Bryn. People call and beg for you still."
"I miss everyone, too."
"Let's get together. Come back for one of our parties. You can bring your toy."

I guessed she meant me. Bryn showed interest without committing to going. She then turned to me.

"Taylor, go wait over on that bench while we talk. Sit with your back straight and your hands on your knees."
"Yes Bryn."

I walked over to the bench. I wondered if she had wanted me to call her Master then. I didn't feel like giving Cassandra the pleasure. I sat with my back straight while the two women talked in the distance. I watched as they walked away in the direction of a coffee shop.

Around thirty minutes later, Bryn came back. She walked past, patted her thigh and said, "c'mon."
I followed.

Six stores, two hours and $500 of my money later we were back in the car.

"Did you have a good time shopping, slave?"
"Yes, Master."
"Do you like shopping?"
"Normally no, Master."
"But you like it with me?"
"Yes, Master."

"Are you worried that I spent $500 of your money, slave?"
"I'm not worried about the $500, but I'm worried about what it may mean going forward."
"Don't worry, slave. I'm not going to bleed you dry. But I do like nice things once in a while, and really I deserve something for all the work I'm doing training you."
"Yes Master."

At home I stripped off my clothes and kissed Bryn's feet.

"You've been very good today, slave."
"Thank you, Master."
"Were you just good because I might let you cum?"
"It was on my mind, Master, but no, it wasn't only that reason."
"What if I told you you weren't going to cum for a month?"

I knew this was dangerous territory.

"I would be sad."
"Sad?"
"Yes. Sad."

Bryn smiled.

"Walk downstairs to the play room and look in the cupboard. There's a curved, thin contraption with screws on the ends. It's brown. Bring it up here. Hurry."

I found the device, which was made of two thin pieces of wood, each a foot long by a couple inches wide. Their middles curved in opposites directions. I grabbed it and hurried upstairs. Bryn had me kneel and removed my chastity cage.

"This is a humbler, slave. Do you know how it works?"
"No, Master."
She held the two pieces of wood together so there was a small hole between them.
"Your balls go between here." She pointed to the hole between the two pieces. "When I fasten the two pieces of wood together, it traps your balls. Sounds great, right?"
"Yes Master."
"You don't mean that."
"No Master."
"But here's the best thing, slave: it goes behind your thighs, so it pulls your balls way back."

She grabbed my balls in her hand.

"Your balls are kinda high and tight, so you're really going to feel it."

She gave my balls a smack.

"With this on, you can't stand up. Most guys need to be on their hands and knees, and they can only move in teeny-tiny steps. That's why it's called a humbler. It also holds your balls out for nice swats with a crop if someone doesn't appreciate all the effort I'm going through to train him, right slave?"

"Yes, Master!"
"Great. Turn around, let's get this thing on."

I turned and faced away from Bryn on my hands and knees. She reached between my legs and pulled my balls back firmly. She tried to get the pieces of wood together over the base of my ball sac, but my balls were in the way. Bryn gripped my balls a little tighter and pulled. I grunted.

"Just a little farther."

She got the wood pieces in place and screwed them together. The wood pinched. The hole didn't feel wide enough for my balls. And even though Bryn had let go, it still felt like she was pulling on my nut sack. It was odd and uncomfortable, until I tried to move, and then it felt like someone was trying to rip my nuts off.

"See," Bryn said, "humbled."

I stayed very still. It was frightening to think that a sudden movement would rip my testicles from my body.

"Slave, I want you to crawl to the other end of the room."

I very slowly lifted one knee and moved it an inch forward. It hurt. I lifted the other knee and moved it forward an inch, even with my other knee. It hurt. Then I tried to move my knee two inches forward and screamed as my testicles almost separated from my body. I went back to one-inch movements. Finally, I got to the other side of the room. Bryn took out her cell phone as she spoke.

"That was good slave. It took you five minutes to get from here to there. We're going to play a game now. You're going to try to cut your time in half on your crawl back to me. If you can make it in two-and-a-half minutes, I'll give you the best handjob of your life. Over two-and-a-half minutes and I beat your ass and balls till you scream and beg for me to stop. Time stops when you kiss my feet. Go!"

She pressed start on her stop watch and held it up for me to see. At first I tried to increase my speed of movement, moving one inch at a time but trying to move faster. This worked for four steps until I moved too much and sent waves of pain through my body. I stopped to let the pain subside.

"Hurry slave!"

I put my knuckles on the ground and pushed up, getting both my knees off the ground at once. I swung them forward and landed with a little smack on the ground. It didn't feel great on my knees, but it didn't pop my nuts off, and getting to cum would be worth a little knee pain.

"Time's running out, slave!"

I lifted up again and swung myself forward. This was going to work – I was making much better time than before. I did it again, then again. I was nearing the couch now. Just a few more swings.

"Come on slave! Faster!"

I pushed up and swung forward once, twice, three times and I was close enough to carefully bend down and kiss her feet.

"Oh, slave!"

Bryn showed me her timer. It read 2:40.

"So close, slave! So very close. I wish I could just give you a hand job, but rules are rules."

Ten fucking seconds! If I had just started sooner I would have made it! Fuck!!! Bryn unscrewed the humbler and my balls gratefully sagged back between my legs. Bryn lifted my head up so that my gaze met hers. Her eyes glowed and she had a bright smile.

"C'mon slave, let's go downstairs and have some fun!"

Say whatever you want about Bryn, but she always kept her word: she beat me till I begged and screamed for her to stop.

Chapter 12

For the next week, things continued on in the same manner. Bryn humiliated me and beat me at will, and I took it and plotted my revenge. Some days I ate her pussy, other days I didn't. Some days I couldn't do anything right and endured about 100 swats with her crop or paddle or cane, other days I only had to take around 50. It was all still humiliating and painful and horrible, but it was getting less so. I felt like that was the scariest thing of all.

Wednesday of the next week, Jen, a student from my seminar, walked into my office shortly before class and handed me an envelope.

"Bryn asked me to give this to you, Dr. Clark."
"Thank you, Jen."
"You're welcome."

I studied her face for any hint of a smile, but if she knew anything about Bryn and my relationship, she kept it to herself. When she left, I opened the letter.

> *Slave,*
> *Tonight I'm going to fuck you.*
> *Love and kisses,*
> *-Master*

Part of me wanted desperately to believe that we were going to have sex. Bryn had complimented me the day before on how well-behaved I'd been, and she even let me sleep out of the cage on Tuesday night. At the same time, this was just the type of psychological game she loved to play: get me excited about a possible reward and then pull it away at the last second. Fucking me could mean anything from a night of wild sex to, well, things I didn't want to think about.

My seminar, the one with Bryn, started in ten minutes. Bryn had timed her letter perfectly to throw me off. I tried to clear my mind and just focus on the class, but every so often my mind wandered back to what kind of fucking I'd get that evening.

In class, Bryn was all wide-eyed innocence, smiling brightly at me and asking a lot of questions. From our talks over the last two weeks, I knew that she knew most of the answers and she was just teasing me. And to make matters worse, she had spent a half hour earlier that day bringing me to the edge of orgasm and then backing away while I drooled like an idiot and promised her all sorts of things if she'd just let me cum. She didn't, of course, and with my hands and legs tied to the corners of the bed there was nothing I could do but thrust and moan and plead. And as the cherry on the sundae, Bryn wore her most revealing top today. I wasn't the only one staring at her tits during class. A quick look around the room found most of the guys and girls sneaking peeks. I felt my dick twitch and try to grow in its tube. I finally split the class into groups of four for private discussion, so I wouldn't have to deal with Bryn.

Class seemed to take forever to end. When it was over, I lied to the class about an important phone call and hurried back to my office and shut the door. Not long after, Bryn came in.

"Take me home. Right now."

Without speaking I gathered my things and rushed out to the car. Bryn walked slower, but I could feel her lust. On the way home, we didn't speak. I stared straight ahead.

Inside her house I couldn't get my clothes off fast enough. Bryn was waiting for me in my room, where she had already removed her panties. She locked my hands behind my back and unlocked my dick, which sprang to attention. I dropped to my knees between her legs and she guided my head to her pussy.

I licked her as if my life depended on it. Bryn lay back and wrapped her legs around me. Every so often her hips bucked and she grabbed onto the back of my head as she screamed.

I lost track of the number of times she came or for how long I was down there. When I was finished, the comforter was wet and my face was covered in her juices. Bryn's breath was deep and steady. She kept her legs around my head, which kept my face pressed against her. I closed my eyes and just breathed. We lay there, contented for a short while. Then Bryn pulled me onto the bed next to her. She didn't speak, she just hugged me.

I cooked a nice meal and we ate in silence. Bryn was smiling, so I wasn't worried I had done anything wrong. And seeing her happy made me happy, too, weirdly.

After dinner I watched a video on cum control and then met Bryn in the upstairs bathroom. She was wearing her black robe. She held a red bag with a long nozzle.

"Slave, do you know what this is?"
"It's an enema bag, Master."

"What's going to happen now, slave?"
"You're going to give me an enema, Master."
"Eating pussy makes you smarter, slave…or at least slightly less dumb."
"Thank you, Master."
"Lie down in the tub and put your feet up on the sides."

Bryn put on rubber gloves and filled the red bag with warm water. She then rubbed some lube around my asshole and inserted the nozzle. She slowly filled me with water. It wasn't painful; I just felt like my stomach was full.

"Hold that in for three minutes."

Again, it wasn't unpleasant, it just felt like I had to go the bathroom.

"I'm going to leave the room while you empty yourself out. When you're done, take a cold shower and clean yourself real well. Then come to the bedroom."

I tried not to think about what was coming. The enema let me know I'd be on the receiving end of tonight's fucking. My body felt tingly, as it does before riding a roller coaster. I concentrated on my breath as I showered and tried to ignore my anxiety. My feet felt heavy as I walked to the bedroom. Bryn pointed to the floor and I knelt between her knees. Bryn handcuffed my wrists behind me and caressed my cheek.

"Close your eyes, slave."

"Now open them."

Bryn had pulled her robe to the side to reveal her dildo.

"Don't look away, slave. Look at it." She grabbed the top of my head and turned me to face it. It was seven inches long and about the thickness of my own dick, which was slightly thicker than normal.

"Slave. I don't want you to be scared. You've had a butt plug in your ass a lot lately, so you should be able to take this. I'm going to be gentle with you this first time but it might hurt. I've got a big dick."

She laughed, and I laughed a little too. It lessened some of the tension.

"I want you to kiss it, slave. Lean forward and give the tip a quick kiss."

"Good. Again . . . good. Now I want you to lick it. Just the tip . . . good boy. You're doing really well. Scoot closer to me . . . good. Keep licking. Start at the base now and lick to the tip . . . good."

Bryn held onto the back of my head and guided me forward.

"Now take it in your mouth, slave. Just the tip. Hold it in your mouth . . . good boy. A little deeper, slave. Not too far down. I don't want you to choke yet. Do you see how the dildo has an attachment at the base that goes into my pussy? When you suck it, it rubs against my g-spot and it feels oh-so good. Keep sucking slave, in and out . . . that's right. Suck my cock."

"Mmmmm, slave, you're a good little cocksucker. I want you to go a little deeper now. You don't have to go all the way down, but you need to learn to deep throat my cock. A little deeper . . . "

Her hand on the back of my head pushed me forward as I felt the tip of the cock against the back of my throat. I gagged and she released me.

"Good boy! That was very good. Again, now. Go as deep as you can . . . good. Now I want you to speed up. You don't have to go as deep, but I want you to go faster."

"Faster slave. You can do better than that. C'mon, you're a cum-thirsty slut. Faster! This cock is all you've ever wanted and you love sucking it; show me! Faster! Get that body into it. Faster you slut!"

She grabbed the back of my head and forced the dildo down my throat. She held tight as I gagged and tried to pull away. After a few seconds she released me and I coughed and drooled. When I looked up at Bryn I expected her to be laughing at me, but she had the same feral look she'd had in the car.

"Get on the bed. Wait! Stand and I'm going to uncuff you. Good. Now on your back."

She tied me spread eagle to the four corners of the bed. I lifted my ass as she pushed a pillow beneath me. She crawled between my legs and poured lube onto her dildo. She rubbed it in and brought the tip of the dildo to my asshole.

"You are not to look away from me or close your eyes. You look right at me until I say stop or I will beat you harder than I've ever done before. Nod yes."

She leaned forward and kissed me. Then she pushed into me.

"Ohhhhh," I'd had butt-plugs in my ass a lot since Bryn enslaved me, but the dildo was wider and longer. I stared deep into her eyes, which were half closed. Bryn snaked her arms under my legs and around to hold onto the top of my thighs. She pushed slowly into me until I grunted in pain.

"Open for me slave. That's right." She pulled out slowly and then pushed back into me until I grunted again. She maintained a slow rhythm, in and out, in and out. All the while I stared into her eyes. She looked beautiful, absolutely beautiful. She pushed farther into me.

"Oh, Master, it hurts!"
She pulled out, then didn't go as deep on her next push in.
"Breathe, slave. Stay relaxed. I'm making you mine. Don't close your eyes. Keep looking at me as I fuck you. Oh, you feel so good, slave. I'm going to speed up now."

She increased her pace. I wanted to close my eyes and escape, but she wouldn't let me. She wouldn't break eye contact with me, and soon I felt my body relax and give in to her. She was going to fuck me for as long as she wanted, and there was nothing I could do but submit. It was like our whole relationship. She was in control and I was her slave. As I came to this conclusion, Bryn smiled, as if she had read my thoughts. She released my thighs and leaned over. Her breasts brushed against my stomach and her hair tickled my chest.

"Kiss me, slave."

I did. Long and deep. She put her hand on my chest and arched her back as she increased her pace even more. Her mouth was open slightly and she was breathing heavy.

She grabbed the bottle of lube and poured some into her hand.

"Do you want me to touch you, slave? Do you want to cum for me?"
"Oh, please Master. I do."

She pulled the dildo out almost all the way, then pushed into me. I arched my back. Then Bryn put her hand on my dick and I forgot everything else. It felt like she was reaching into my soul. With a few strokes I was close to cumming, until I remembered the cum control techniques I'd been practicing and started breathing deeply and sending the energy through my body. It was too much though. It felt too good and it'd been too long since I'd cum. I felt the orgasm gathering in my balls. I started to buck.

Bryn was close to cumming too. She moaned and arched her back.

"Are you going to cum for me, slave?"
"Yes, Master! Please Master!"
"Cum for me slave! Cum now!"

Bryn and I came at the same time. I screamed and shot ropes of cum into the air as Bryn threw her head back let loose a primal scream. My hips bucked as my dick shot jet after jet onto my stomach. Bryn kept stroking me, milking every drop from dick. I shivered as waves of pleasure shot through me. It was the most intense orgasm of my life.

When it was over, Bryn pulled out and lay down beside me. She ran her fingers through my hair and held me close to her.

"You’re shaking slave. Are you ok?"
"I'm wonderful, Master."
"Let's rest for a bit."
"Yes, Master."

Chapter 13

Over the next two weeks, Bryn became more strict in my training: finding fault in almost everything I did. I wasn't bowing quickly enough; my posture showed a bad attitude; the kitchen wasn't clean enough. I had thought that after what had happened in my bedroom that she would calm down a bit, but it was as if I had graduated into a higher, more difficult level of servitude. Bryn was almost impossible to satisfy, and despite the improved morale, the beatings continued.

Bryn continued to drill me: barking orders and positions. If I hesitated for a second, she'd break out the wooden paddle, or - worse - the cane, and mete out quick, hard punishment. She also said I had to improve my stamina, so she began leaving me in uncomfortable positions for long periods. On Monday, I stood on my tip-toes holding a ping pong ball against the wall with my nose. On Wednesday, I stood with my arms outstretched, holding a tray with a plastic cup of water in each hand. I was to hold my arms out for 30 minutes, and if I failed, I would receive one stroke with the cane for every minute left before 30. I lasted 4 minutes.

But while she was strict and harsh, she was also loving. She let me massage her and worship her pussy almost every day. And we spent a lot of time on my bed, kissing, with her telling me how happy she was with my progress.

Her control of my time increased. In fact, it had never gone back to normal after she had set up an hourly schedule a few weeks back. I had my entire day planned out, save for two hours at night when I could work out and an occasional night off to see some friends. On one hand, I got a lot more done now that I had a definitive start and stop time to my work. On the other, I spent most of my days either uncomfortable or in outright pain.

I knew better than to complain, or at least I thought I did.

On Saturday morning, I made Bryn breakfast and then ate my own oatmeal mix from a bowl at her feet. I then watched a video on massage: this one specializing on the legs, and massaged Bryn for about an hour. After I was done I knelt. I had to pee.

"Master?"
"Yes, slave?"
"May I go to the bathroom?"
"No. Down."

I knew Bryn was testing me, waiting for me to get impatient so she could beat me. I waited, forehead pressed to the floor. I heard her open a magazine. After maybe five minutes, she spoke:

"Slave, kiss my feet."

I went to work on her feet.

"Do you still have to go the bathroom?"
"Yes, Master."

She went back to her magazine.

"Slave?"
"Yes, Master?"
"Recite your slave pledge."

"You are my Master and I submit to you. My purpose is to serve you and make you happy. I will obey your commands immediately and without question. I worship, obey and fear you. By accepting your will as my own, I am a better and more content person. Without you I am lost and unhappy. Please accept me as your slave, and do with me as you will."

Bryn went back to reading. After five more minutes, I really had to pee. I rocked slowly back and forth.

"Slave, what are you doing."
"I have to go the bathroom, Master."
"Is that attitude in your voice, slave?"
"No Master, it's that my bladder is hurting and it's creeping into my tone. I apologize if it sounds like attitude."
"It does. And you're being ungrateful this morning so you don't get to do everything you want the exact second you want it."

"Are you sulking, slave?"
"I do what you ask, Bryn! You tell me to kiss your feet, and I kiss your feet. How is that being ungrateful?"
"Slave, crawl closer."

She lifted my chin with her finger.

"First, you address me as Master, not Bryn. That one's going to cost you. And yes, you kiss my feet when I ask. You grudgingly kiss my feet as quickly as you can so you can be done with it. I let you lick my ass and massage my feet and you grudgingly do those, as well. I told you at the beginning of all this that I wanted to be worshipped, obeyed and feared. You obey me, Taylor, and you fear me. But you don't worship me, me. Not truly. If you did, you would see that kissing an owner's feet is a privilege that not every slave enjoys. I know some dommes who barely let their slaves touch them."

I took a deep breath in, then released it.
"I will call you Master. I will do whatever you want. But please don’t tell me you’re doing me a favor by blackmailing me."

Bryn’s face tightened. She stared at me for a moment as she took her own deep breath.

"Go ahead and pretend you're an unwilling victim, Taylor, if that makes you feel better. But you practically begged me to enslave you. You're not an idiot; you knew that I was getting into your head, but you kept coming back for more. And it didn't take much to get you doing whatever I wanted."

"You’re blackmailing me, Master. You beat me when I don't do everything you say!"

"I beat you a little! I've heard of other slaves who spent weeks being beaten before they'd kiss their owner's feet. You did it right away! The beatings were for your fragile psyche, to give you an excuse to do everything you’re afraid to admit you want! You're a slave, Taylor! You've got a slave's mentality. I didn't create it; I just brought it out. And you're too stupid to see that you're happier now than you've ever been."

"Nothing to say to that, slave?"

I didn’t answer.

"Go to the bathroom and then downstairs."

I don't know how Bryn had managed to make not letting me go to the bathroom into proof that I was an ungrateful slave and a reason for punishment, but she did. It occurred to me that she was just waiting for me to get upset. I would have to do better. She wanted me to slip up so she could punish me. I'd have to pretend to follow her every rule as closely as possible and keep my cool even when she prodded me. I'd be the perfect slave for her, until I had my chance.

Downstairs, I knelt before Bryn and kissed her bare feet. She wore the dildo that went inside her and massaged her g-spot. She took my chin in her hand.

"You want to show that you worship me, Taylor, this is how you do it. Worship my cock. There's no honey or pussy juice on it now. It's just my cock. I want you to make love to it. The more you do, the better I feel. You want me to feel good, don't you slave?"
"Yes Master."
"And you want me to know that you worship me, isn't that right slave?"
"Yes Master."
"Good, I'm going to give you some motivation." She leant down and unlocked my cock from its cage. It sprang to life. "Now make love to me, slave. Make love to my cock with your mouth."

I knew I was going to get a harsh beating if I didn't do a good job, followed by having to suck her dildo again, so I might as well save myself a beating. I thought about the best blow job I'd ever gotten, from a Japanese girl about three years ago. I leaned forward and slowly kissed the tip. I looked up at Bryn and held her gaze as I took the base of her dildo in my hand. I kissed it again, slowly, letting my tongue come out to lick the underside below the tip. Bryn exhaled a soft moan.

I slowly kissed down the underside of her cock. Then I began to lick it. I kept eye contact with Bryn. I licked it up and then down again, then blew on it slowly. Finally, I took the dildo in mouth and slowly worked my way down. Then I sucked up the dildo and let my lips trail over the head as I came almost all the way off. Bryn stroked my hard cock with her foot.

I worked a steady rhythm up and down. I experimented with the firmness of my lips to see how I could get the biggest reaction from Bryn. She liked medium firm, so medium firm it was. I sped up a little. When I looked up at Bryn she had her eyes closed and her mouth open.

I grabbed the base of the dildo and began to stroke it. Bryn let out a moan.

"All the way down, slave. Take all of me in your mouth."

Bryn held on to the back of my head and gave me a little push. I went all the way to the base of her cock and gagged and coughed. Bryn rubbed my dick with her foot.

"That's right slave. That's good."

I deep-throated her again. When I looked up at her, her eyes were bright. She grabbed my hair and pulled me off of her.

"Turn around, all fours."

Bryn squirted lube on her finger and pushed it inside of me. She was breathing heavily. She brought her dildo to the base of my asshole and pushed the first few inches inside. She didn't speak; she just worked her dildo slowly in and out, pressing a little deeper every third of fourth stroke. I put my head into my hands and tried to stay calm and open. Bryn pushed almost all the way inside me, which made me gasp and try to struggle away, but she held me against her as she moved her hips in a circle. Then she pulled almost all the way out, stopping with the head of the dildo just inside my asshole, then pushed in again slowly. She did it again, not going as deep but increasing her pace. She did it again, then again, always pulling almost entirely out before plunging into me. She was grunting and digging into my hips with her nails. I heard her orgasm coming about a minute out. She made a deep guttural sound that grew louder and louder until she exploded with a yell, driving her dildo into me.

She stayed inside me, not moving, for another minute, as I stayed with my head against the floor. The she pulled out and walked in front of me, placing her foot in front of my face. I imagined I was kissing her lips and passionately, slowly, kissed her foot. I kept on kissing her until she bent her knees and patted my head.

"That's what I mean by worship, slave. *That's* what I want *all the time*. You've still got punishment coming for not addressing me properly, so get yourself together and lock yourself face down on the bondage bed. You've got five minutes."

I was on the table in four minutes, but Bryn made me wait for another twenty. When she came back into the room, she stood over me and rested her hand on the back of my head.

"What's my name?!"
"Master."
"You called me Bryn upstairs."
"I'm sorry Master, it was a mistake."
"Yes it was. Let's help you not make that mistake again." She showed me the finger of ginger she was holding. It was mostly peeled and had been cut into the shape of a tiny dildo.

"This is going in your ass. From what I hear, it stings a lot. When it does, remember how you address me and what your place is."
"Yes, Master."

She pushed the ginger in my ass. At first I felt nothing, and I hoped that maybe this wouldn't be so bad. But I knew that was wishful thinking. Soon enough I felt a tingling sensation in my ass, which quickly grew to burning. My asshole was already raw from her fucking me, and now it felt on fire. I twitched and jerked on the bed, and my asshole kept involuntarily clenching, which only intensified the burn.

"What's my name, slave?"
"MASTER! IT'S MASTER!!"

Bryn grabbed the base of the ginger root and shoved it in and out of me a few times, which just made everything hurt worse. I was trying desperately to calm down so I could unclench my ass, but I was trapped in a vicious circle: it burned so I clenched, which made it burn more, which made me clench more, which made it burn more, and on and on. Bryn walked to the wall and grabbed a cane. She came back and knelt in front of me, taking my face in her hands.

"You did a good job sucking and taking my cock, so I'm going to go easy on you. But not addressing me by my title is a lack of respect, and I won't have that. So you're going to get punished. Understand?"
"Yes, Master."

She walked behind me. I wanted her to hit me. The stinging pain of the cane would take my attention away from my burning ass. Bryn stood behind me, slowly rubbing my ass with the cane but not hitting me. What was she waiting for? Why wouldn't she hit me?

She knew! She knew I wanted the cane just then to take my mind off the burning sensation. I tried to stop myself from squirming, but it just made me squirm more. Bryn tapped on the ginger root with the cane.

"Please, Master!"
"Please Master what?"
"Please beat me with your cane!"

But she didn't. She kept tapping on the ginger root or running the tip of the cane up and down my legs and balls. I don't know how long it took for the burning to go down, but it finally did. I felt my body relax onto the table.

WHAP! WHAP! WHAP! WHAP! WHAP! WHAP!

"What's my name!"
"MASTER! You're name is Master!"

WHAP! WHAP! WHAP! WHAP! WHAP! WHAP!

"I don't-"

WHAP!

"want"

WHAP!

"to have to remind you"

WHAP!

"ever again!"

WHAP!

"Clear?"

WHAP! WHAP! WHAP!

"YES MASTER!!! IT'S CLEAR MASTER!"

WHAP! WHAP! WHAP!

"Good. Why don't you stay here and think about it for a little while."

She turned the lights off on her way out. I lay against the table catching my breath and once again marveling at the incredible sadism of my owner, at how she was able to read me so perfectly to do exactly what would hurt me the most.

Chapter 14

The next two weeks were more of the same, though there was some good news as well. A paper I'd written was going to be published in Psychology Today, and I had already been booked on two different morning shows! On top of that, I had finished three more chapters for my book on influence and the manipulation tactics of cults. Maybe it would help just a few people avoid throwing their lives away.

Serving Bryn grew less difficult, not because she was any less demanding, but because things just get easier if you keep doing them. It seemed normal now to walk around in front of Bryn wearing only my cock cage. I found that the more focused I was on serving her and performing each task I was assigned, the easier those tasks became. If I had to worship her feet, I really concentrated on worshipping her feet. I stopped thinking about how demeaning it was, because all that did was make the time go slower and the task worse. If I focused on pleasing her, things went smoothly.

Bryn showed more care for me as well. She noticed the effort, and while she wasn't any more lenient with me, she gave me more pleasure: soft caresses and kisses. She started massaging my prostate every few days. I had heard about prostate massage, and I'd even had a woman try it on me once, but I hadn't liked it. Apparently, she just hadn't been any good at it. When Bryn did it, I felt shivers of pleasure all through my body. She usually teased my cock as she did so, though she always stopped just before I came. I had been her slave for six weeks and I'd only orgasmed once. Today, Bryn slowly worked one hand up and down my cock while the other played with my prostate. As usual, I was tied spread-eagle to the bed.

"Slave, would you like an orgasm?"
"Yes, Master."
"Do you think you've been a good slave?"
"I do, Master."
"And good slaves deserve to cum."
"Yes, Master."
"So you're a good slave?"
"I believe so, Master. If you say so."
"And what does a good slave do after he cums?"
"He falls asleep, Master."

Bryn laughed, thankfully. She sped up her strokes and I felt my orgasm rumbling closer.

"I don't know Master. He's grateful. He brings his Master to many orgasms?"
"Does he leave his mess everywhere?"
"No, Master, he cleans up his mess."
"That's right."

She played with the underside of my cock, right below the head. I arched my back. She rubbed in small circles with the tip of her finger.

"So you're going to clean up your mess for me, slave?"
"Ohh, yes Master."

My whole body shivered. Bryn gripped my cock and pumped her hand hard.

"Say you're going to clean up your cum for me!"
"I'll clean up my cum for you Master!"

I was at the point of no return, my hips were bucking and I wouldn't be able to hold back.

"With your mouth."

I exploded onto my stomach, giant ropes of cum. Oh my God it felt good! I spasmed as Bryn kept pumping me until my dick turned so sensitive that I twitched and moaned. Bryn smiled, gave me two more painful pumps, then let go.

I was breathing hard. I wasn't looking forward to eating my cum, but I was going to have to do it. My guess was that cum tasted terrible.

"My sweet slave. You make the most adorable faces when you cum. Now what did you promise me you'd do if I let you cum?"
"I'd clean up my mess, Master."
"How?"
"With my mouth." I hadn't actually promised anything, but I knew where that argument would end. Bryn made circles with the cum on my chest with her finger.
"There's a lot here. I hope you're hungry. Open."

She scooped up a finger full. As she brought it to my mouth, it started to drip, and she made it just in time. I closed my mouth and sucked my cum off her finger. It tasted disgusting, really disgusting.

"Don't make that face, slave. It's good for you."

She scooped up some more and held it over my open mouth as it dripped off her finger. Then she coated my lips with what remained. Slowly, she fed me my cum until it was all gone.

"What do say, slave?"
"Thank you for letting me orgasm Master. And thank you for feeding me my cum."
"You're welcome slave. Why don't you savor the taste while I go read. I have a lot of reading for my psychology project. My teacher is such a hard ass."
"I've heard he's a real jerk."
"He tries to act all tough and macho, but on the inside he's just a sweet little boy who wants to be told what to do."
"Only by the right woman, though. He's got very high standards."
"I would hope."

She stood up and patted my cheek. Then leant over and gave me a soft kiss on my lips.

"You make me happy, slave."

I let out a deep sigh of contentment and lay back on the bed. I realized I was smiling.

I knew what Bryn was doing. I'd spent the last twelve years studying cults and indoctrination procedure. I knew why Bryn was keeping me exhausted, beaten and dehydrated. I knew why she was mixing pleasure and pain and alternating between being loving and cruel. I just felt that I was stronger than that. The people who get taken in by cults *want* to be taken in by cults. Mind control doesn't work unless you let it work. I just wasn't going to let it work. I'd let Bryn think it did, and I'd do what she said, but eventually she'd get bored or something would happen where I'd get my freedom back. Until then, handjobs were better than getting my ass beat.

Chapter 15

The semester continued on. Bryn was as strict as ever. She kept me guessing constantly. Some days she was loving and I spent long periods worshipping her body. Other days she was cruel and would find any excuse to beat me. I stopped being surprised at her shifts in moods and just took them as they came.

Two and a half months into my slavery, I was cooking Bryn dinner and massaging her feet with my hands and my mouth. I was getting better at judging her reactions, so I could switch up before she got mad and corrected my technique with a heavy hand. Bryn had taken off my chastity cage and was teasing my cock with her foot.

Bryn was loving it, and I was enjoying seeing her happy. And her foot playing with my cock wasn't bad either.

And then the fire alarm went off.

"Shit! Sorry Master!" I ran to the kitchen. I'd been making garlic bread as an appetizer and forgotten about it in the toaster-oven.

I disconnected the alarm, then opened the windows in her kitchen and got most of the smoke out. When I came back to the living room, Bryn was sitting with her arms crossed.

"Slave, go into the drawer of the side table and get my hairbrush."

I got it.

"That's the one. Now bring it here and get over my knee. You just earned a spanking."

My mouth went dry. I tried to focus on my breath, but the room seemed to bend and contort. Memories of Natalie came rushing back to me.

"Slave! Over my lap."

I felt in a daze as I positioned myself over Bryn's lap. She spread her legs and clamped them over my dick.

"I can't believe all this time together and this is your first over-the-knee spanking!"

I concentrated on breathing.

"What's the matter?"
"Nothing Master. I'm fine."
"Are you sure?"
"Yes, Master."
"No, you're not. Tell me what's going on…right now." She raised her hand and brought it down hard on my ass. I came. I didn't even know it was possible to cum that quickly. It felt like my dick had been plugged into a pleasure socket.

"Holy shit!"
"I'm sorry, Master."
"Holy shit!"
"I couldn't control it, Master! I'm sorry!"
"Kneel."

I sat on my heels in front of her and stared at the floor between her feet. My face was flushed with embarrassment.

"What was that?!"
"I don't know, Master."
Bryn lifted my chin so my eyes met hers. It hurt to look at her.
"Yes you do. What's going on?"

And so I told her about Natalie and how she spanked me and sent me to the corner. About how I still masturbated to the memories and how ashamed I felt that I wanted it to happen to me. I hadn't planned on telling her anything more than what had happened when I was ten, but once I started talking it was hard to stop. Several times I almost broke down crying, and I had to stop to gather myself. What the fuck was happening to me?! When I was done, I stared at her feet. I just wanted to disappear into the earth. My breath was ragged. Bryn put two fingers beneath my chin and raised my head up to look me in the eyes. She leaned forward and kissed me on the lips.

"Come up on the couch."

Bryn hugged me close to her, then put my head in her lap. She stroked my hair.

"It's ok, Taylor. It's ok."

I couldn't hold back. The pressure was too much and I thought I would explode. I cried. She had beaten me with a cane and paddle and every type of punishment device I could think of for two and a half months. She had put sports rub on my cock and balls and locked me in a cage and kept me hungry and thirsty and slapped my face at will. And yet it was this act of tenderness that caused me to lose control. I put my head in her lap and cried large heaving sobs. She held me and stroked my back.

"It's ok to want something and be ashamed of it, Taylor. We're all taught there's only one way to be when we're young, and we believe it, even when it means hating a part of ourselves. Wanting this doesn't make you wrong or less of a man."

Bryn kept rubbing my back and speaking soothingly:

"You can be who you are with me, Taylor. You don't have to hide your desires and your needs. I'm here to take care of you and lead you and give you the discipline you crave. You're safe with me."

She kissed me and held me close to her "You're safe with me, Taylor, you're safe."

Chapter 16

I wasn't sure how to act for the next week. All I wanted to do was not think about what had happened with Bryn and what it meant. Did I want to be her slave? I couldn't. I loved my life before she took control of me and now I was trapped and blackmailed into doing whatever perverted thing she wanted. But sometimes it felt good. But it wasn't my choice. But . . .

Round and round my thoughts went, each time making no progress and leaving me dissatisfied and confused and just wanting to stop thinking about it. So I buried myself in my work and my tasks for Bryn. Whoever had painted her living room had gotten paint on the outlets, so I took them off and cleaned them. No one had cleaned the drains in the bathroom upstairs in a while, so I cleaned those, too. I had research to do for my book, so I researched everything that could possibly help me. And it helped. I stopped thinking so much about what everything meant and who I was.

When Bryn saw how I had cleaned off the outlets and cleaned the bathroom, she undid my chastity belt and put me over her knee. She began slowly rubbing my ass.

"I know you want a spanking, slave."

My dick throbbed.

"Beg me to spank you slave."

She began moving her knees up and down, massaging my dick.

"Master, please spank me."

"That wasn't very convincing. Beg."

She moved her knees a little faster.

"Please Master! Oh, God, please spank me!"

She stopped moving her knees and spanked me hard and fast. I thought I might cum, but I did my cum control techniques and stopped myself. When she was done, Master had me stand in the corner. After 15 minutes, I stood before her. She gripped my chin in her hand.

"Are you going to be a good boy for me?" Her hand snaked down and grabbed my cock. She started stroking slowly.

"Yes, Master."

She stroked faster.

"You'll do everything I say."

I could barely speak.

"Yes, Master."

"Look at me." She took her hand off my chin and held it in front of my dick. "Be a good boy and cum for me! Cum for me now!"

I shot my load into her hand. It was so intense I almost passed out. Bryn continued to stroke me until I was empty.

"On your knees slave. Lick up your cum from my hand."

"Yes Master."

Two Fridays later, I was kneeling between Bryn's knees. I hadn't cum since our little role-play.
"Slave, I'm leaving town for the weekend with some friends. I'm leaving this afternoon and I'll be back Sunday night. I haven't made a schedule for you. You're going to be your own master for these next two days.
"You don't have any rules for me, Master?"
"No, slave."
This seemed like a trick.
"Thank you, Master."
"You're welcome, slave."
"Are there things you want me to do?"
"Sure. I want you to eat your food on your knees out of your dog dish on the floor, without using your hands. And I want you to not use the furniture, except when you're working on your book. But I'm not telling you to do that. The only thing I want you to do is written on this piece of paper." She handed me the paper.
"Thank you, Master."
"I'm taking your car. You can walk wherever you need to go."
"Yes Master."
She pulled out the key to my chastity belt and placed it on the coffee table.
"I'm going to leave you this key to your chastity cage. If you want to take it off and masturbate, it's up to you."
"Thank you, Master."
I looked at Bryn as she studied me.
"Master?"
"Yes slave?"
"You're ok if I masturbate while you're gone?"
"I'm not saying that, slave."
"So you don't want me to, Master?"

"I'm not saying that either. It's your choice, and I won't be upset either way. You get to decide what you want to do based on what you think is best for our relationship."
"Thank you Master."
"I'll see you in a couple days. I expect you to be kneeling by the door when I return." She looked at her watch. "We have a couple hours before I leave. Let's get that tongue working and give you something to remember me."

By the time Bryn left my tongue was sore and my face was covered in her juices. Bryn patted me on the head, told me to be a good boy, and closed the door after her. I heard my car drive away, and then I felt very alone. It was odd: I had been living by myself for a long time before this period of enslavement. Now being alone felt very strange, as did not having rules.

Next to the key on the coffee table was Bryn's note. I opened it.

Slave,
I want you to enjoy your weekend off from slavery. At the same time, I do want you to remember me. So you're going to wear the butt plug that I've left on the kitchen counter three times a day for an hour each time. Go get it, along with the lube and a rubber glove.

I did. It was a slightly larger butt plug than I was used to. It also had a leather belt attached to it.

No doubt, you've noticed that you've graduated to a larger size. Congratulations! It has a nice leather cinch so that you don't have to worry about it falling out. Isn't that wonderful? Right now, here's what you're going to do:

1. Collect butt plug, lube and a glove.
2. Put on glove.
3. Pour lube on finger.
4. Slowly insert finger into asshole.
5. Take out finger.
6. Pour lube onto butt plug.
7. Insert butt plug into asshole.
8. Attach cinch through legs and around waist.
9. Think fondly of me as you go about your day :)
I'll be back before you know it.
Kisses,
Master

The only way I was going to insert my own butt plug was to do it quickly and not think too hard about it. So on went the glove and the lube. I tried shoving the plug into my ass from behind, but my asshole wouldn't open. I tried breathing deeply and relaxing, but no luck. Finally I put the butt plug face up on the floor and gradually lowered myself onto it. My asshole unclenched and with a few adjustments it was cinched inside me. I fastened the belt. It felt uncomfortable, but I was getting used to uncomfortable.

I looked at the key on the coffee table. I could be masturbating in no time. All I had to do was grab it. My dick started to grow in my chastity tube, thinking about the non-stop jerk off session I was going to have for the next two days. But something didn't quite feel right about it. Bryn knew I'd masturbate. She said it was fine, so it wasn't like I'd be doing anything wrong. It just didn't seem like the right idea right now. Instead, I went and worked on my book. I had been making good progress and figured I might as well ride this wave of productivity. After an hour I took out the buttplug and got back to work.

The next thing I knew it was 9pm. I had really made good headway into a difficult chapter about counter-indoctrination procedures. I put in the buttplug and made myself a chicken breast and broccoli. I put it on a plate. Bryn wouldn't know if I ate out of the dog dish, and she didn't really expect me to, anyway. So why did it feel like cheating? I stood holding the plate in my hand for about a minute and a half, unable to get myself to just walk into the living room and put it on the table. What was wrong with me? Had Bryn gotten inside my head? No. I just wasn't totally sure she hadn't rigged some camera, and it was better to be safe than sorry. With a sigh I poured my dinner into my dog dish and ate it hands-free from the floor.

After dinner I removed the butt plug and did some stretching before crawling into my cage and falling asleep.

Saturday I went to the gym and worked out for almost three hours. It felt fantastic. At home I put the butt plug back inside me, then watched another pussy eating video and did my tongue strengthening exercises. Then I stared at the key to my chastity cage until I decided to watch the next video on cum control. Why didn't I just take the key, take off my cage and masturbate? I don't know. If there were cameras in the house, Bryn had hid them well, because I didn't see any. At one point I even reached out to grab the key, but I didn't actually touch it. Instead I worked more on my book and wrote out a lesson plan for my classes.

On Sunday I decided to clean the house to keep myself busy and keep my thoughts off masturbating. First, though, I walked to the florist and bought some flowers for Bryn's return. I thought Bryn would be pleased with me for not masturbating, and I thought I could make her extra happy by making her home spotless. I got some paint and touched up some spots on the walls. Then I dusted everywhere. I got rags and cleaners and started the moldings throughout the living room. I cleaned under the fridge. I swept and then mopped the floor. I even polished the handles and hinges to all the doors. It kept my mind occupied. A couple times, I heard cars going down the street and thought maybe Bryn was home. After each time, I was struck by the irrational thought that she wasn't coming home and that I'd get an email telling me she'd moved on. I knew that was ridiculous: this was *her* home, after all. But I didn't feel like trying to reason out an irrational thought, so I just let it go.

The third time was the charm. The car I heard coming down the street slowed, then pulled into the driveway and stopped. I had finished cleaning and showering and I was naked except for my collar. I raced to the door as I heard the car door open and close, and then the sound of her heels on the driveway. My heart was racing. Why was I so nervous?

When the door opened I snuck a quick look at her face and dove to worship her feet. A knot of worry in my chest unclenched. Her feet felt wonderful, and kissing them felt better than I wanted to admit. Bryn leaned down and ran her hands over my back, down to my butt, then up my sides to my face.

"Up."
Bryn walked around her apartment, checking the cleanliness.

“Slave, I’m pleased with you. The flowers and the house look beautiful.”
“Thank you Master. I missed you.”
She came back and stood above me. She held my face in her hands and smiled wickedly at me.
“Did you have a fun weekend masturbating?”
“No Master.”
“You didn’t masturbate?” She smiled even wider.
“Whyever not?”
“I wanted to make you happy, Master.”
I leaned back, giving her easy access to my balls.
“You can check, Master.”
Bryn didn’t check. She looked right into my eyes. Her smile faded and turned to astonishment.
“You’re telling the truth! You didn’t even try!”
“No Master.”
She was impressed…and something else. She looked over at the key on the table, then back at me. Finally, it hit me.
“Master, that’s not my chastity key, is it?”
“No it is not.” She shook her head and smiled. “I spent the whole weekend imagining the moment you realized.”
“I’m sorry to have spoiled your fun, Master.”
“Don’t be sorry, slave, that’s what punishment is for. Come.” She patted her lap. “Over my knees.”

What followed was a slow, sensual spanking. Master hit me hard, but never too hard. In between spanks, she rubbed my ass and told me how pleased she was that I’d been such a good boy, and that she knew I was going to continue being a good boy for her. I was in Heaven. Afterward, I knelt between her legs. She leaned back on the couch and closed her eyes as I brought her to orgasm after orgasm.

Chapter 17

Two evenings later, I returned to Bryn's to find a silver Mercedes in the driveway. Inside, there was an attractive, well-dressed woman who looked to be in her late forties or early fifties – though wearing it well – sitting with Bryn in the living room. There was a pot of coffee and two cups in front of them.

"Slave, this is Ms. Martina. Say hello and address her as Ma'am."
"Hello Ma'am."
"Hello Taylor." Her voice was deep and friendly. She was very dignified. Hearing me called 'slave' didn't surprise her.
"Clothes off, slave. Martina's one of us."

I unbuttoned my shirt slowly while trying to read Martina. She wasn't surprised by seeing me undress or by the fact I was wearing a chastity cage. I crawled to Bryn and kissed her feet.

"Slave, I want you to crawl to Martina and kiss her feet as well. You're to tell her that her wish is your command. Then crawl back to my side and kneel."

I crawled to Martina and kissed her feet.
"You're wish is my command, Ma'am."

Martina ignored me. She told Bryn that everyone missed her, which was the second time I'd heard someone say that. She talked about how business was going well and how there were many slaves who still called about her. From her tone, it was clear that Bryn looked up to Martina, and I could see why. She radiated poise and calm command.

Eventually, I made dinner for the three of us. Bryn let me sit at the table, and Martina asked questions about my research. She knew a little about my work, which was flattering. When I tried to ask about her work, she just smiled and redirected the conversation back to me. She wasn't rude or condescending. She obviously knew what was going on, and I bet she knew a lot of the specific things Bryn made me do, but I didn't see judgment in her eyes. I had a feeling she could be a real bitch when she needed to, but that she preferred getting along with people.

When Martina left, she hugged Bryn goodbye. Then she looked at me and waited. I sank to my knees and kissed her feet. She told Bryn she'd see her soon and left.

Bryn read on the living room sofa as I did dishes. When I was finished I kissed her feet. She reached down and petted my head.

"Master, may I ask you something?"
"What is it, slave?"
"Were you a dominatrix? And was Martina the headmistress?"
"Yes, slave. That's where I worked between high school and college. I actually started working there my senior year of high school."
"That's where you learned how to control people."
"That's where I refined how to control people. I knew a great deal before I started working for Marty. That's why I learned so quickly."
"Master, is Martina the same Marty you were talking to on the phone in the car the first time I drove you home?"
"Aren't you smart! Yes, that was Marty."

"And so that was all part of the set up. You wanted to see how I reacted when you dominated someone in front of me."
"Yes. And you got a big erection and tried to hide it from me."
"I thought I did."
"There are ways to tell when a guy wants to hide that he's turned on. You have no idea how obvious you were."
"What did I do that gave it away?"
"Those are my secrets, slave." She was wearing a short skirt. She lifted up her hips and pulled down her underwear to her feet, then stepped out of them. "Why don't you worship me for a while and think about how lucky you are to serve me."

Chapter 18

Winter break came and I took Bryn to Paris. There I was still her slave. While I got out more, Bryn was very clear about how I should stand and walk and comport myself. She created hand signals to use in restaurants to indicate when I could eat and drink. Through Martina's connections, Bryn – or I guess both of us – had the use of a local dungeon, and any mistakes I made during the day were corrected there at night. One day, upset at my behavior, she left me in the hotel room handcuffed in the closet with a dildo in my ass for four hours.

Despite her strictness, we grew closer. Paris is a romantic city, and Bryn and I let that romance bring us together. It feels strange to write that about someone who'd been enslaving me for months, but it was true. We never ran out of things to talk about, and she acted more or less like my girlfriend when we walked around the city. We held hands; we kissed a lot; we watched the sun set from the Eiffel Tower, her leaning into me as I held her around the waist.

Every restaurant we went to, the maitre'd told me how lucky I was to be with such a beautiful woman. I felt reenergized being away from home, and the week flew by all too quickly.

Our first night home, Bryn made me sleep in my cage. I made the mistake of asking why, so she took me downstairs and beat me with about a dozen different implements. I slept in the cage the next night, as well. This time, though, I kept my mouth shut.

Two days before the start of classes, I came home from working at my office to find a candlelight dinner waiting for me. Bryn was dressed in one of the dresses I'd bought her in Paris, and she looked like a Goddess. I'm not sure how, but she grew more beautiful every day. As we ate, she gave me loving glances. I knew something was on her mind, but I knew I should just wait. She'd let me know when she was ready.

After we were finished, I got up to do the dishes.

"Don't do the dishes."
"No, Master?"
"No, slave. Come here and carry me up to my room."
"*Your* room, Master?"

She didn't speak. She just nodded slowly. I scooped her into my arms and walked up the stairs. I had never been allowed in Bryn's room before.

It was beautiful. It was warm and cozy, and it was done in the same good, expensive taste as the rest of the house. But because it was *her* room it was like I'd been granted admission to somewhere secret and forbidden and wonderful. Bryn never took her eyes off me.

"Put me down on the bed."

I gently put her down on her king-sized bed.

"Take my dress off, slave."

I did.

"And my bra and panties."

I knelt before here and removed her shoes. I felt the urge to kiss her feet, but Master hadn't ordered me to do that.

I pulled off her panties and removed her bra. She sat up and ran her fingers through my hair.

"Kiss me here." She pointed to her left inner thigh. I gave her a long slow kiss.

"And here." She pointed to her right inner thigh. Another kiss.

"Here." She worked her way up her legs, and soon I was licking her slowly. I paid attention to her breath and soon she was dripping wet and moaning.

"Stop slave."

"Yes, Master."

"Take off your clothes."

I was naked in fifteen seconds. Bryn grabbed the key to my chastity cage and unlocked me. I grew hard immediately.

"Kneel."

She took my face in her hands and kissed me.

"Make love to me slave. I want to feel you inside of me."

When I was eighteen, I went sky-diving. I kept my cool when the plane took off, right up until it was my turn to jump. Suddenly, every molecule of my body buzzed with excitement. I felt hollow and filled with electricity, and I could barely think. That's how I felt now as I moved between Bryn's thighs. I looked into her eyes as I slowly entered her. I went in halfway before drawing almost all the way out. I moved my hands up her sides and over her breasts as I pushed back into her, a little deeper this time. She sighed and gripped my sides. We kissed a long slow kiss. She ran her hands over my chest and down to my waist as I made love to her. I felt her muscles constrict around me and I concentrated on my breathing like the cum control video had taught me. I pushed fully inside of her, and Bryn gasped and arched her back. I kissed all over face and her hair. Soon we were moving in unison.

"Look at me, Taylor."

I stared into her eyes as her eyelids fluttered and she softly came. I kept moving in and out of her. She started breathing heavily. She dug her nails into my back as I sped up my pace. I was pushing into her as far as I could go. She felt wonderful, and I knew I would orgasm soon. I wanted to wait for her so we could cum together. She was getting closer. I concentrated on what the video told me and relaxed the muscles around my balls.

Bryn came loudly. And my body went rigid as I felt the most amazing orgasm take hold of me. I screamed and bucked my hips as we gripped each other tightly.

We lay in each other's arms breathing heavily. I couldn't speak. I couldn't think. It felt like our bodies were becoming one. I waited for my erection to go down, but it didn't. It suddenly occurred to me I'd cum on the inside, without ejaculating. All those cum control videos had paid off! Bryn sensed it, too.

"Nicely done, grasshopper. Rest against me. We can start again soon."

We made love all night. In the morning I held Bryn against me tightly.

"I love you, Master."

She smiled at me.

"I love you, too, Taylor."

I made Bryn breakfast. I wanted her to know that I didn't think our relationship had changed, just because we'd had sex, so I only put her plate on the table. Bryn sat at the table and just said, "down, slave." I waited with my forehead pressed against the floor while she ate.

After breakfast, she dictated my schedule for the day, including what I could eat and drink. She was more generous with food and water now that I was behaving properly.

Chapter 19

The Spring semester started. I was only teaching two seminars, one that was continuing from the fall. It was a lighter schedule class-wise, but I worked harder than I'd ever worked before. I didn't have a choice in the matter, of course, as Bryn set a strict schedule and demanded detailed reports as to what I'd done and how much I'd accomplished.

I finished my book a month before my deadline. My editor was in shock. She called me Friday night to tell me it was excellent. I took Bryn out to celebrate. At home, I took off my clothes at the door and kissed her feet.

"Slave, I'm going to give you a choice. I want to reward you for finishing your book, so I was thinking about making love to you."

I waited.

"But then I thought, I haven't tortured you in a while. Yes, you've been good, but that good behavior has robbed me of the joy I receive from punishing you. You know I'm a little bit of a sadist, don't you slave?"
"A little bit, Master."
"I want to please you, but at the same time, I'd rather take you downstairs and torture you. I'm going to let you choose, though. Do you want to make you happy or me happy?"

"Master. I exist for your pleasure, not my own. I want to make you happy, and if that means torturing me, then please, take me downstairs."

Bryn smiled playfully, then rose on her tiptoes to kiss me on the mouth. She grabbed my chastity cage and led me downstairs by my dick. In the dungeon, she handcuffed me to a chain hanging from a bolt in the ceiling. She put a stool between my legs and adjusted the height so that when I was flatfooted, my balls rested on the seat. On my tip-toes, my balls were just clear. She took off my chastity cage, then put a plate with white powder on the stool. I stayed on my tiptoes.

"Have you ever felt itching powder before, slave?"
"No Master."
"Oooh. It's rough."

She put on a rubber glove and rubbed a bit of powder onto my arm. Within ten seconds I felt it. It burned like poison ivy!

"You're going to want to stay on those toes, lover. Your balls are much more sensitive than your arm. And if you hop around it might even get on that pretty cock of yours."

She smiled.

"Can you last on your toes for five minutes, slave?"

I had thought when she said torture she was just going to beat me with a cane. That I could have taken without complaint. But this was crazy! My arm felt like it was being stung by a thousand fire ants.

Bryn clapped her hands.

"That look! That's exactly what I wanted my pet!"

She showed me the timer.

"Just four minutes and forty-five seconds left."
"Thank you Master."

Bryn stripped down to her bra and panties and sat in her chair facing me. She called out the time every twenty seconds, knowing that it would make it go slower. I concentrated on my breathing. If I could stay calm, I could get through this. I worked out a lot and my calves were strong.

"One minute left, slave!"

My legs were shaking. They weren't cramping yet, but I knew I didn't have much longer.

"Forty seconds slave!"

I put all my attention on the top of my head. It was cool in the room, but I was sweating.

"Twenty seconds!"

I was going to make it. Even if I cramped up now, I could ride it out.

"Five minutes! You did it, slave!"

Bryn came forward and kissed me on the lips, then went back to her chair.

"Now let's see if you can do five minutes more!"

After another minute the cramps came. I started moving my weight from one foot to the other, trying to get some relief. It worked, kind of, at least for another minute. But after that I was done. My legs slowly gave way and my balls fell into the plate of itching powder.

I've heard people say that the few seconds before the pain starts are the worst. Who ever says that is lying. The anticipation is bad, but the itching was unbearable. I begged Bryn for mercy. I pleaded with her. But she just smiled and rubbed her nipples as I twisted and screamed.

After ten minutes of complete agony, Bryn let me down and took me to the shower. The relief was immense. When I was dry, I kissed Bryn's feet.

"Thank you Master for letting me please you."
"You're welcome, slave."

Bryn took me to my bedroom and tied me face up to the four corners of the bed. She put clothespins on my nipples and whispered in my ear.

"Do you think your cock still works tonight slave?"
"I don't know Master."

She kissed slowly down my body till she got to my cock. I got hard.

"Your penis has recovered, slave."
"It still hurts a bit Master."
"Poor penis."

She gave it a slow kiss.

"You were so giving tonight, slave."

As she spoke, I felt her breath on my dick.

"You were so brave."

She licked my penis from the base to the tip. I moaned.

"Poor slave. Doesn't even know he's a masochist."

She took me into her mouth and moved slowly up and down. I sank into the bed.

"Thank you Master!"

Her hair tickled my thighs. She pressed the tip of her left index finger against my asshole as she continued.

"Thank you Master!"

Bryn pulled off her panties and climbed onto the bed. She sank down onto me, cumming right away as my cock hit her cervix. She rolled her head and pulled off the clothespins from my nipples. I screamed.

She rode me till we were both exhausted.

Chapter 20

Towards the end of Spring semester I was notified that I had received tenure! I had been pretty sure I was going to get it, but the relief was immense. I had almost dropped out of college at one point. I had gone through times when I felt like I'd never amount to anything. And now I was a tenured professor at a respected university.

Amy the department secretary made me a cake and gave me a big hug.

"I'm so happy for you Dr. Clark!"
"Thank you Amy. How's the boy?"
"He's great." She stared at me as if debating whether to say something. I guess she decided it was a good idea. "You know, you've changed Dr. Clark."
"Really? How?"
"Well, don't take this the wrong way, but you were always a little arrogant. But as this year's gone on, you've gotten a lot nicer, a lot more down to earth. Whatever you've been doing has been good for you."

I wondered what she'd say if she knew.

Bryn was ecstatic. She made me a big dinner and gave me a celebratory over-the-knee spanking. Afterwards she let me eat her pussy for half an hour. I offered to let her torture me, but she took me up to her bedroom instead and fucked me with her strapon. Then she mounted me and we made love all night.

That Friday night, we were in my car on the way to a party. Bryn wouldn't tell me much, other than we were going to meet some of her friends from her days as a dominatrix. She seemed tense about going and lectured me as we drove:

"At this party there are going to be lots of couples like us. You're to be on your best behavior. You keep your eyes on the floor at all times and speak only when you're spoken to. If a woman tells you to do something, you do it. The only exceptions are if she tells you to do something sexual or something dangerous. Other than that, you're a lowly slave, and slaves do as they're told. Is that clear?"

"Yes Master."
"Address every woman as 'Ma'am,' clear?"
"Yes Master."
"At this party, I'm going to let Cassandra take care of you for a little while."
I didn't like how that sounded but knew better than to complain.
"Yes Master."
"Won't that be nice?"
No.
"Yes, Master."
"So I should leave you with her all night, slave? You'd prefer to serve her?"
"No Master, I prefer to serve you. But if I have to serve Cassandra to serve you, I'll happily do it."
"Yes, you will."

If I had somehow found this party a year ago, I would have been shocked speechless. It was in the basement of some club, and the room was filled out with with plush couches and torture equipment. There were cages and spanking benches, stocks and whipping posts.

It was full but not crowded. There were women in all sorts of fetish-wear: corsets, fishnet stockings, thigh-high leather boots. Some were holding crops; a few were holding whips. It was almost entirely couples, with the females fully clothed and the men either naked or dressed up as sissies. Some men had already upset their owners, because they were being beaten while a crowd watched. One man crawled after his mistress as she walked, keeping his nose pressed against her ass. Every once in a while, she would take a sharp turn, causing the man to lose contact and fall over. When he did, she beat him with a cane.

There were private rooms as well, and I saw some groups head into them.

I wondered how many of these men had been blackmailed into this lifestyle and how many had come by choice. I knew a lot of guys craved to be made into slaves, but it still seemed strange to throw away your freedom when you didn't have to. I looked at one man as he moaned in ecstasy while his mistress whipped him. At one time I would have been shocked and disgusted, but now I didn't think much of it. It was just a guy who liked to be whipped getting his needs met.

"Slave!"
"Yes Master."
"Keep your eyes down! What did I tell you?"
"I'm sorry Master."

Bryn stopped a woman walking by who was carrying a cane.

"Excuse me, my slave is way out of line. May I borrow your cane?"

"Of course, dear."

Bryn looked sternly at me.

"Foot!"

I knelt on the floor and pressed my lips against her foot. Bryn gave me 10 sharp cracks of the canc, then handed it back to the woman.

"Slave, kiss this woman's feet to thank her. What's wrong with you?"
"Sorry Master. Thank you Ma'am."

I kissed her feet. She walked off.

Bryn saw Martina and the two embraced. I got them drinks and waited on my knees as they talked. Martina didn't acknowledge me, which I somewhat expected.

"Slave, I need to talk with Martina in private. Let's go find Cassandra."
"Yes, Master."

Cassandra was sitting on a couch with men standing on either side of her. She was wearing bright red lipstick and a tight-fitting corset that she all but spilled out of. She looked like a porn fantasy, but beneath her sexy, cool veneer I sensed a petty, immature woman, jammed full of entitlement and anger. And I'd bet money that she was terrible in bed.

Bryn and Cassandra kissed and talked for a little while. Apparently, my temporary placement with Cassandra had been agreed on beforehand. Bryn handed her my leash and gave me a stern look.

"You are representing my training. Anything less than perfect behavior means I am way too lenient with you. You won't like the results."
She grabbed my chin and lifted my eyes to meet hers. "And have fun."
She patted my cheek, then kissed Cassandra and walked off. Cassandra looked down at me with a big shit-eating grin on her face.

"Kiss my foot, slave."
"Yes, ma'am."
"Not just the top, idiot. Kiss the bottom. Lick it."

I did. I knew this would not be a pleasant stay with Cassandra, and the only way I could see to keep myself from Bryn's wrath would be to do just as Cassandra said. I figured she'd find any excuse she could to punish me.

"Would you like to lick my ass, slave?"
"I'm not allowed to ma'am."
"I didn't order you to lick my ass, stupid. I asked you if you wanted to lick my ass."
"Since that would be breaking one of Master's rules, I don't, ma'am."
"What if it weren't one of her rules?"
"I don't know, ma'am. I can't think about it as anything other than her rule."

I had hoped this last response would anger her, and it did. She wanted to trip me up and make me say something wrong, but she wasn't smart enough to do it. The conversation continued like this, with her asking me dumb questions and me answering them honestly and in ways that pissed her off. She made me get her a drink then beat me with a crop because I supposedly got her order wrong. She kept trying to get a rise out of me and kept failing. I could feel her losing her temper.

"If you were my slave, I would have you gagged all the time. I'm going to recommend that to Bryn. What do you think of that?"
"I do what my Master orders. What I think doesn't matter."
"You're so full of shit."

I kept silent.

"You don't feel you're being disrespectful, do you?"
"I didn't think I was being disrespectful, Ma'am. I'm sorry if it came across that way."

WHAP! WHAP! WHAP!

The crop slashed against my ass.

"You think I can't sense your disrespect? I'm going to make you my slave and really train you. I don't think you'll have that attitude after three weeks with me."
"Yes, Ma'am."
"Come sit next to me."

She ran her finger down the side of my face.

"Can you imagine what it would be like to be my slave? To be bound and gagged at all times, locked in a closet until you learned respect?"
"Yes, Ma'am."

SLAP!

"That wasn't an answer. My question was, can you imagine it?"
"It's impossible for me to imagine being anyone else's slave but Master's, ma'am."
"Really?"

She smiled. She looked cruelly happy.

"But what are you going to do when you're sold to someone else?"

This caught me off guard.

"I'm not going to be sold, ma'am."

Cassandra put on a look of fake pity and held my chin in her hand.

"You really haven't figured it out yet?"
"I haven't figured out what, ma'am?"
"What do you think Bryn's training you for?"
"To be her slave, ma'am."

Cassandra laughed her shitty laugh.

"You? Bryn's personal slave?" She laughed again. "You poor fool. You really think you're going to be her slave? That's adorable."

I kept quiet.

"Idiot, Bryn is a Goddess. She can have her choice of any man she wants. Why would she choose a lowly professor when she could have a hedge-fund billionaire or a movie star?" She looked at me like I was an idiot.

“She's training you for sale you stupid twat. That's what she does."

I stared straight ahead. This was bullshit. Cassandra was a cunt.

“Wait, don’t tell mc. Martina did a home visit recently? And she had dinner with you and asked you about yourself? Gee…I wonder what that was about?”

“I don’t know, Ma’am.”

“And now here you are, in public, serving another Mistress who also knows Martina. Quite a coincidence!”

She licked her lips.

"Bryn is our best trainer. She's trained five slaves for us over the past few years and they've all brought sizable sums at sale. You're going to be sold. That's what Bryn and Martina are talking about right now. Martina wants to know if you're ready for sale, and Bryn is probably telling her yes. Have you slept together?"

"What?"

SLAP!

"Address me correctly."

"What, Ma'am?"

"Have you had sex? Bryn has sex with her slaves when they're ready for sale. It's like their graduation ceremony. You have! Oh, you poor dear. I can see that you’re in love with her. And you thought she was in love with you. Men are so stupid. You, my arrogant, handsome fuckwad, are about to be sold."

She couldn't be telling me the truth. But there was something different about her tone. Earlier, when she was trying to trip me up, she sounded desperate, as if she didn't quite believe what she were saying. But now she seemed totally sure of herself.

"What's the matter, professor? You look upset. Where'd the smartass answers go?"

I stared down at the floor.

"Did you really think she'd be satisfied with you?"

SLAP!

"I said, did you really think she'd be satisfied with you?"
"Yes, Ma'am. I did."

"Then you're even dumber than you look. I can't believe you didn't figure it out. Her other slaves did. I guess they weren't as full of themselves as you are. You really are the perfect fool. And you're not enough to satisfy her."
"If I were sold, who would I be sold to, ma'am?"
"How should I know? You'll be put on auction and someone will buy you. Then you'll serve him or her."
"Him?"
"Yes, him. Many of our slaves go to male owners. Bryn's been training you for it, hasn't she? You've sucked on her dildo, right? And she's fucked you in the ass, too, I bet. What do you think that's for? She's training you to please a man."

She shook her head in mock sadness.

"Poor slave. Everyone's sad when they leave Bryn. But you'll get used to serving someone else after a while. I'm sure you'll miss your career. Maybe your owner will let you keep it, but I imagine you'll have to give it up."

The world felt like it was collapsing around me. Cassandra drank it up as only a miserable, shitty, emotional vampire could. I wanted not to believe her, but I couldn't deny that it made sense. Had it all been a set up? Bryn appeared out of nowhere as a transfer student and made me her slave. Was it really all just an act?

Cassandra gave me a ton of commands which I carried out with emotionless efficiency. She found reasons to beat me, but I barely felt the crop. She didn't have the technique Bryn had to really hurt me physically.

Fifteen minutes later, Bryn came and got me. Cassandra gave me a bad report, saying I'd been disrespectful and lazy. She made some things up. I stared at the floor. I felt Bryn's eyes on me, but I didn't look at her.

"I'd take him to the stocks and let us all have a chance to punish him if I were you."
"That's a good idea, but unfortunately we have to go."
"Oh, no! Why? You just got here."
"We have a big day, and I really just wanted slave here to meet the local scene."

I heard silence, and I knew that Bryn had changed some previously agreed upon plan.
"Ok, sweetie. Take care."

I kept my eyes down and walked behind Bryn to the entrance, where I retrieved my clothes. Bryn took off my collar and we walked silently to the car. I felt heavy and sick. I sat silently as Bryn drove.

"Slave. What's going on?"
"Sorry Master."
"What are you sorry for?"
"I don't know, Master."
"Taylor. What's wrong?"

I didn't know where to start. I couldn't bear to hear it if it were true. If it were all a set up. If I had been an even bigger dupe than I thought.

"Taylor? Talk to me."
"Cassandra told me."
"Cassandra told you what?"
"Bryn, are you going to sell me?"
"What?!"
"Cassandra said you were just training me to sell me. She said that's what you do."

"Did she?"
"She said you've done it before."
"And you believed her?"
"I didn't want to. But a lot of what she said made sense."

Bryn was silent. I was afraid to think about what her silence meant.

"Do you really think everything I've done and said has just been an act?"
"Master…Bryn. You're better than me at this."
"At what?" She was upset.

"You're better at . . . you're smarter than I am. You can make me do what you want! I was under your spell form the first time I met you. You turned me into your slave so easily."
"So you don't believe anything I say or do?!"
“Please just tell me the truth, Bryn. I can't bear not knowing. If it's true-"

"Shut up."

I shut up.

"I'm not selling you."

Relief flooded through me. My head didn't feel like a weight was pulling it to the floor. I still felt worried, though. When Bryn spoke next, her voice was gentle.

"How could you think that?"
"She seemed so sure of herself."
"You probably pissed her off with your quick wit, so she decided to go where she knew she could hurt you."
"Well, she did."

"You didn't consider that Cassandra was lying to get you upset?"
"You manipulated me to make me your slave. It’s not crazy to think that maybe this was just more manipulation. And she knew about some of the things you made me do."
"Yes, well, we talk and share ideas and methods. Cassandra's quite smart."
"Really?"
"Yes."
"*Really*?"

"Yes, and if you don't want me to lend you to her for an entire week, you'll stop acting so surprised."
"Sorry."

We drove for a while in silence.

"Taylor, do you believe that I'm not preparing you for sale?"
"Yes, Bryn."
"I can tell when you're not being fully honest with me, slave. Remember I have that superpower."
"I want to believe it. But I'm just worried."
"And my word's not enough?"
"Master, you wanted honest. I'm being honest. I didn't say I was being rational. Cassandra said that you always have sex with slaves before you sell them. And she said that you and Martina were talking about my sale right then."

Bryn laughed.

"God, Cassandra really is a bitch, isn't she?"
"Yes, Bryn."
"I've trained slaves before, but it was always agreed upon by all sides beforehand. They weren't just sold to a random highest bidder. Everyone involved was heavily vetted."

I was silent.

"Taylor. What kept you from running away from me at the beginning, before you admitted you wanted to be a slave?"
"My reputation. My career."
"Right. And what would happen if I tried to sell you to someone?"

I hadn't even thought of that point.

"I wouldn't serve them."
"Exactly. You'd be worthless as a slave and Marty's reputation would be hurt. You *could* be kept locked up and eventually broken - I mean *really* broken, like made insane, but that's not what Marty's about. And I wouldn't let that happen to you. Despite your personality, I like you."

I tried to smile, but I couldn’t.

“Are you crying?”

I was. A small laugh escaped through my tears.

"Taylor, you don't think I care for you? You can't tell what's real emotion?"
“I thought I could. But I don't know, Bryn. Cassandra said you could have anyone you wanted, and it's true. You could. You could have a movie star or a billionaire, so . . . "
"So what do I want with you?”
“Yes.”

She stared ahead for a moment.

“You're right. I could have just about anyone. At least, I've never not gotten someone I wanted. But answer me this: you've fucked a lot of good-looking women, right?"
"Yes."
"And did they make you happy? Were you satisfied?"
"No."
"No you weren't. Because there was no connection. Trophy fucks are good for a little while, but for long

term we all want someone we connect with." She looked over at me. "We connect, Taylor. I felt that the first time we met."

I was feeling a lot better, but I was still in emotional turmoil. Bryn reached over and put her hand on mine.

"Taylor, you're a charming, smart, handsome guy. And you're a genuinely good person. Sometimes you're even funny. What do you think I'm looking for in a guy? Money? I have that. Fame? I don't care about fame. I want someone who makes me happy, who truly wants to be my slave. That's you. And don't pretend you don't want to be my slave, because what's going on now proves it. Think about it, you must have known that you weren't going to serve anyone else. So why were you so upset?"

I had been staring at my hands not speaking for some time. I kept at it.

"You were upset because you *want* to serve me. You may not love it all the time, but deep down you *need* to be my slave. No one else has ever made you feel as content as I have, and it's because I control you. I told you that you were a slave; you just needed to find the right owner, and that's me."

She let that sink in for a little while.

"I want to hear you say it."

As we pulled onto Bryn's street, everything suddenly became clear. She was right. She was the only woman I'd ever felt content with, and I had done everything she asked. I told myself it was because of her blackmail or to avoid getting beaten or to lull her into a mistake, but it wasn't. I did it because I wanted to. I needed her control, and serving her satisfied something that had been missing my entire life. I'd been afraid to admit it, but I loved her and I loved being her slave. I kissed her hand.

"Thank you Master."
"For what?"
"For making me your slave."

Bryn smiled.

"I do want to be your slave, Bryn. I love you, and I want to make you happy. And I want to marry you."
"Whoa! Did you just ask me to marry you?!"
"Yes Master. Will you marry me?"
"I'm the dominant one in this relationship, mister. If we're going to get married, I'll tell you."

She pulled into her driveway and turned to me.

"Getting married won't change anything, Taylor. You'll still be my slave and I'll be as sadistic as ever. Your orgasms will belong to me and you'll sleep in the cage when I want you to. We may eventually have kids and a white picket fence, but they'll always be a dungeon in the basement."

"Oh Bryn, I wouldn't want it any other way."

She stared at me without smiling. I took a deep, nervous breath.

"Slave?"
"Yes, Master?"
"We're getting married."

"Master, I-!”
“Shut-up.”

“Not right away: when I graduate. In the meantime, we should probably rework the vows, huh?"
"I'll get to work on them right away."
"Not right away. Right away we should head upstairs, don't you think?"
"Yes, Master."

The End

Printed in Great Britain
by Amazon